I0680950

DARK RIDES
Volume One

Erotic Disney
Theme Park Adventures

by

Blu Carson

ISBN: 978-0-9910079-4-3

Published by Dark Rides Press, a Bamboo Forest Publishing imprint
First Printing: December, 2014

Visit us Online at:
www.bambooforestpublishing.com

Dear Reader,

Dark Rides is an erotic journey of sexual adventures, intended as a tribute to the world of fantasy created by the Parks and Resorts of Walt Disney World. To enhance the pleasure of readers, a themed cocktail pairing is included with each story. Please relax and enjoy this experience meant to stimulate both mind and body. Welcome to my Dark Rides.

xoxoxo

Adventures

We Want The Redhead
The Pirates of the Caribbean

CAPTAIN'S RUM RUNNER
Resort Shared Drink Menu

1 oz. Captain Morgan Original Spiced Rum
1 oz. Blackberry Brandy
1 oz. Creme de Banana
3 oz. Orange Juice
3 oz. Pineapple Juice
Serve Over Ice
Add a float of Myer's Dark Rum

DISNEY CAST MEMBERS have always been my favorite kind of people. Most say that they enjoy their job working for "The Mouse". They understand my obsession with Disney and even encourage it. Even outside of their roles on property, Cast Members are a different breed of human, and I like them! I always make a point to talk to them simply because I enjoy the conversation.

So, it was no surprise that during a trip with friends to Hollywood Studios during *Star Wars* Weekends in May, I found myself in a long conversation with an extremely handsome, young, male, Cast Member from New York City. His name was Jake, he was in the Disney College Program, and he hoped to stay for good. He said he really enjoyed working there and planned on a long career with Disney, slowly moving his way up the ladder. He was definitely my kind of people!

As with most Cast Members, he had a bright smile and a sweet, charming, good-guy look. He wasn't very tall, maybe 5'8"? He had dark hair, dark eyes, and, surprisingly, a beard. Despite Walt Disney having sported a lovely mustache during his lifetime, the Walt Disney Company had strict rules for facial hair on Cast Members. When I questioned him about the Disney rules, he said that as long as it was trimmed close and kept very neat, it was allowed. He looked great with it;

it gave the illusion that he was a few years older. He told me that he didn't want to be treated like some "punk kid," and the beard helped avoid that.

Jake had very broad shoulders, and I could tell that he worked out. In fact, during our conversation, he mentioned that as much as he loved going to Disney's fancy signature restaurants, he could never go to Victoria & Albert's. When I asked him why, he explained that he was "too muscle-bound" to wear a suit jacket. That cracked me up, but he was very serious. He admitted that unless he bought a tailored suit, he couldn't wear one. He had a great body; it was obvious that he worked hard on it. I was tempted to reply that I also have a similar problem due to my huge tits. Unless I wear a very constrictive fitted bra, keeping them from spilling out of my dress is nearly impossible. But, I didn't want to offend his young ego.

Most of the park Guests had already filtered over to the *Fantasmic!* theater for the first show of the night, so the Carbon-Freeze Me experience where Jake worked was dead. He and two other Cast Members were having lightsaber fights when we stopped to talk. Their impromptu battle was what made me take notice of Jake immediately. They must have practiced every night, because they spun and jumped like professionals, putting on a convincing show. We talked long enough that one of my friends suggested we all take some pictures together. I felt like a tourist, but once Jake slipped his arm around me to pose for the picture, I realized that my friend had the best idea *ever*!

It was almost time for the second *Fantasmic!* show, and Jake was closing the Carbon-Freeze Me experience for the night. I rarely stayed in Hollywood Studios late enough to see *Fantasmic!*, but, since I was there, I decided that I might as well. The second show of the night never had a full audience. I said goodbye to Jake and the other Cast Members, but before I walked away, Jake asked me to wait. He said he had something for me. He ran inside the attraction entrance, then returned quickly with a few small objects. Where Jake worked, Guests who purchased the 3D image of their own faces on a Han Solo frozen body received a free *Star Wars* logo wristband with a blinking light. The items were only available during *Star Wars* Weekends and not for sale separately. If there was one way for Jake to win my heart, it was with collectible Disney merchandise!

I thanked him over and over as I became giddy and lost all focus on flirting. The only things that could keep my mind off of Jake's strong shoulders and fantastic body were the gifts, so when he casually asked me to send him the pictures we had just taken, I gave him my phone while I played with the wristbands.

We said our goodbyes and Jake flashed me the most mischievous smile as I walked off to the show. The glimmer in his eye made me wonder if the attraction was mutual. It was all that I could do to restrain myself and not ask him to come home with me that night.

During the *Fantasmic!* show, my phone vibrated. When I checked it, I was surprised to see that it was a text from Jake.

"Nice pigtails."

As I've gotten older, I've become much more bold in expressing my sexual desires. I recently learned to accept my status as a cougar. I no longer waste time when I see something I want. I wanted Jake.

"Thank you. They also make convenient handles," I texted back.

Jake responded with a selfie showing him standing in his bathroom wearing nothing but a towel. He had three colorful Dia de los Muertos skull tattoos on his upper arm that accented the curve of his muscles. Aside from the tattoos, I couldn't stop staring at the sexy V peeking out of the top of the towel. I missed most of *Fantasmic!* while looking at the picture and imagining pressing my body against his smooth, tanned, skin, and then ripping that towel off of him with my teeth.

When I had talked to him earlier, he mentioned that he had tattoos, but I never saw them. They were covered by his clothing. It was a shame that tattoos were another "no, no" for Cast Members, because he and his tattoos looked damn sexy. His bad-boy sexiness was far from the image the Disney Company had in mind.

I sent him a picture of me in return. It showed me wearing a black and purple corset that laced up in the front. It pulled my breasts tightly together until they were nearly overflowing out of the top. A small detail of curled, black, lace trimmed the edge and was just enough to cover any bit of nipple that may show when I moved.

"Wow! They're nice."

"They?"

"I meant, IT. It's a nice pic!"

His flub made me inappropriately laugh during one of the semi-quiet moments in *Fantasmic!*. I may have felt embarrassed had I not been having so much fun flirting with Jake.

I left the park that night without seeing him again. For the next few weeks, we flirted back and forth in texts. We discussed meeting during my upcoming birthday trip. I booked a room at Saratoga Springs for the night, but my plans changed at the last minute and we didn't get to see each other that visit. We still talked now and then, but never made any specific plans to get together after that.

Then, one night in the fall during the start of the Food & Wine Festival in Epcot, I was walking over the bridge that links France to the UK. The bridge was crowded with Guests waiting to view *Illuminations*. I felt a tug on my pigtails from behind and spun around, prepared to smack a drunk creep. There he was! It was Jake!

He grabbed hold of me in a big bear hug and nuzzled his fuzzy, bearded-face down into my neck. He let out a low, sultry moan into my ear as he held me tightly. His yummy sounds made me laugh, especially since I was easily amused after just finishing a passion fruit and mango margarita from La Cava del Tequila.

He felt so good that I couldn't resist sliding my hands up under his shirt. I drunk-giggled a bit as I attempted to publicly fondle him. *Illuminations* had just started, so I was not concerned if anyone noticed my wandering hands. I was so happy to finally see him in the flesh again, instead of just in his teasing semi-naked texts.

"I saw pigtails go by and then looked closer and realized, *I know her*!" he said.

"Yeah, I'm your pigtail girl."

He tugged on my hair as he continued to hug me.

"You're right, they *do* make good handles," Jake joked.

I squirmed around against him. We both laughed and he let me go.

"So, now that I finally caught you again, can we hang out? My brother is here visiting me." Jake pointed to his brother. I could vaguely see the back of his head as he stood along the railing of the bridge watching *Illuminations*. "I'm off the next couple of days. He won't mind if I ditch him for a little bit tomorrow. What are your plans?"

"Yeah, I still feel bad about cancelling on my birthday. That won't happen again. Tomorrow I want to go to the Magic Kingdom. I've been craving some raping, pillaging, and plundering of redheads by my favorite pirates. Oh, and a Dole whip!"

"That sounds like a perfect first date to me! I'll wear my hook and eye patch."

"Mmmmm, *sexy*!"

Jake pulled me back to him in another warm embrace.

"I'd love to take you home with me now, but I have to go hang with my brother."

"It's okay, Jake. I'm heading out now to beat the crowd before *Illuminations* is over. We can play pirate and wench tomorrow."

He leaned down and gave me a quick peck on the lips. I felt entranced by the scent of his cologne, which lingered in the air as he pulled back from me and smiled down.

"Exit gift shop of Pirates, tomorrow evening."

"I'll be there, darlin'. Enjoy the visit with your brother."

We hugged each other tightly one last time and then I continued over the bridge towards Future World to exit.

I intended to spend the entire next day relaxing in the Magic Kingdom, but I arrived there later than I had expected. I have never been a morning person, so there was no point in forcing it. I arrived mid-afternoon and headed straight for Liberty Square to Sleepy Hollow for the messiest-but-most-worth-it snack at the park, the Nutella and fresh fruit waffle. It was my new favorite indulgence. I ate it slowly and savored every last sweet bite while I enjoyed my view of Cinderella Castle. Luckily, I had just missed the castle show and three o'clock parade. They were cute, but if I heard one chorus of *Celebrate You* it would have stuck in my head for days.

After my waffle, I made my way through Frontierland, where I stopped and shot air rifles in the Shootin' Gallery. My dad always propped me up there as a kid, and I still liked to go play there sometimes. I always felt a strong sense of satisfaction in hitting a target and watching something in the haunted graveyard move or pop up.

After my moment of playing Annie Oakley, I headed to the exit gift shop at Pirates of the Caribbean. It was always a madhouse. I was looking through a rack of silly pirate-themed t-shirts when I felt a tap on my shoulder. I instinctively turned around and a pair of strong hands took hold of either side of my face. Then, a warm mouth met mine for a full-on, deep, knee-buckling kiss. It was Jake. I must have looked like a deer in headlights after his greeting.

"I hear it's good luck to kiss a princess."

"Hmmm. You probably should try it again to test the

theory. It seems like an important cause for science."

He took my face in his hands again and gently kissed me with just a light peck. After his initial greeting, a quick kiss was not going to satisfy me. I took hold of his shirt and dragged him towards me as I walked backwards to a spot behind a rack of shirts. He smiled from ear to ear and followed along. As soon as we were hidden, his hands went down my body and gripped onto my ass. Our lips met, and then our tongues. He held me tightly and I pressed my fingers into his back as we devoured each other. Finally, I had him in my grasp!

We broke free of the kiss and both let out a contented sigh. A *real* kiss was a small "fix" to relieve the sexual tension that had built up between us.

"That was much better," I said, while still catching my breath.

"Yes, much. Now that we both feel better, would you like to look around the store?"

"That is *not* the first activity that comes to mind right now, but we can give it a shot."

Jake laughed and took my hand to lead me out from behind the clothing rack. We walked around the gift shop, talking and flirting.

"How's the visit going?"

"It's cool. My brother and I just play video games and drink most of the time. Sometimes we go out to the House of Blues. It's fun to party there."

I could not stop myself from touching him as we walked through the store. My fingers seemed to constantly drift to his muscular arms or broad chest each time I tried to direct his attention to something in the shop. Still, as much as I wanted him right then, I enjoyed spending time with him in the Magic Kingdom.

"And work?"

"It's good now. Not as much fun as during *Star Wars* Weekends when you were there. I still have Guests asking me to do the impossible every day. Everyone wants to know how to get to the front of the line for Toy Story Mania or how to get a special meet 'n' greet with their favorite character. I don't know what they want me to do."

"But they deserve it, Jake," I teased.

"Yeah, they deserve a Goofy shoe in their asses. They get pissed off, too. It's unbelievable sometimes."

"Sounds magical."

"My name tag should say, 'Where Dreams Come True... and Get Crushed Too'."

"Jake, that is *so* mean! But, hysterical!"

"I love my job."

"So, when are you gonna take me on that special backstage tour you keep promising?"

"As soon as I lure you over to my territory, I'll give you the full VIP experience."

From all of our text conversations, Jake knew that *anything* backstage-related turned me on. I had no shame in being a Walt Disney World groupie. Even just walking around a shop in my favorite place in the world with my sexy, new friend made it extra special and excited me more than I could hardly stand.

As we walked around, I noticed that some people were playing the new Pirate's Adventure interactive game in different places in the shop.

"Jake, have you tried the Pirate's Adventure game?"

"Not yet."

"Some parts of it are actually really cool."

I pointed to a curio cabinet on the side of the shop. It contained model ships. Red lights glowed, shots fired, and one of the ships "sunk" into the cabinet.

"That was cool," said Jake. "All that's missing is a red-headed wench tied to the mast by the pirates."

Jake ran his hand through my red hair. My eyes closed and a wave of warmth rushed down over me.

"It looks like a fun game, but do you know what I would like right now?"

I opened my eyes and glanced at him curiously. "A Dole whip?"

"Maybe later. Right now what I would like is for us to go ride Pirates together. I'm in the mood for a red-headed wench," he continued to fondle my long red hair, twirling a lock of it around in his fingers. "Would you like to go for a ride?"

"A red-headed wench ride, huh? That sounds like a new attraction upgrade that I would enjoy. I suppose that it's a good thing that today is No-Panties in the Park Day."

"Oh, it is?"

His eyes looked down over my body. He smiled and tilted his head slightly as if he was trying to see through the fabric of my dress. I clasped my hands behind my lower back and lightly swayed my hips back and forth, teasing him as my dress flipped around.

"Yep, new thing. It's a rule. I think it's just in the testing-phase, but I'm hoping that it catches on."

"Yes, I would definitely support that as a new park enhancement."

We walked out of the shop and turned right, towards the attraction entrance. I still always looked up to the top of the wall at the entrance each time I was there, hoping that the talking parrot would be back. He never was.

It was a slow day in the park. Everyone must have been at Epcot for the Food & Wine Festival. We wound down through the queue of cold stone and cement walls. We could hear a few voices echoing up ahead of us but there was nobody around.

Jake took the opportunity to pin me to the wall. Once again our lips met. The heat of his body, scent of his cologne, and taste of his kiss distracted me from the rough texture of the wall as my back slid up and down against it. He wasted no time in lifting my skirt and sliding his hand underneath and between my legs to check for panties.

"No, you *don't* have panties on. You are *such* a naughty, little, wench aren't you?"

"Yes! Yes! I'm a *very*, naughty wench!" I gasped.

We heard some voices in the corridor and he released me from the wall. I took a moment to get my sea-legs back before following him. I felt wetness on my inner thigh as I walked; Jake was pretty good at encouraging my naughty wench side.

We made it to the ride loading area, and there were only a few people waiting. They were directed to the front of the boat, and we were seated in the back. Jake stepped into the boat first, and I followed.

As soon as the boat set sail, he pulled me close against him.

"Come 'ere ya brazen wench."

His left arm went around my back and he placed his right hand on my thigh. I laughed and moved in closer to him. As we traveled through the first scene of the ride, I could feel the bottom of my sundress slowly being raised inch by inch by his right hand. Once it was above my knee, I placed my hand on top of his.

"Jake, there are people in the front of the boat."

Jake's hand went under my dress and between my thighs.

"Then you should probably try to be quiet."

"I knew you were going to be a fun new friend."

I straightened my dress so that it covered Jake's hand and adjusted myself in the seat. I leaned against his chest and spread my legs further. He started kissing me gently as his fingers began teasing my pussy lips. I squirmed around in the seat as I felt his fingers spread me open a bit.

"A warm, wet pussy to play with on the boat? Now *this* is a ride refurb that I can support!"

Our boat turned the corner towards the ride drop. Jake pressed the tips of two of his fingers inside me.

"Hold on, Princess."

As our boat plunged down over the falls, his fingers plunged into me and I yelled out, but, thankfully, so did the other people in the front of the boat!

The boat leveled out at the bottom of the drop and floated through the path of cannon fire. I bit my lip as his fingers stroked deeply inside me. With each burst of water from a cannon that spurted up next to us, he pushed his fingers in deeper. We turned the corner to see the animatronic mayor tied up and dunked in a well. Water sprayed from his mouth each time his head raised back up to the top of the well.

"He's almost as wet as you," Jake whispered into my ear.

"Please don't make me squirt like that here!"

Jake laughed and continued to play with me as we went through each scene of the ride. Luckily, I had seen it hundreds of times, because on this trip, I was not able to pay it much attention. However, Jake never had a problem taking it all in. He kept finger-fucking me while he looked around, and spoke casually as if nothing was happening.

"Look at the poor kitties…. Gotta love the happy drunk pigs…. Those red-headed wenches are worth every penny," he rambled.

He was not distracted in the slightest, yet, the ride could have really been on fire and I wouldn't have noticed!

I pushed my hips towards his hand gently. I didn't want to get too carried away and have anyone in the front of the boat turn around. I have to say though that nothing was more awkward than being in the throes of passion, tossing my head back, looking up, and seeing a dangling, dirty, hairy, nasty, pirate animatronic foot in my face as we went under the bridge!

As we moved into the room with the dog holding the jail cell key, Jake slid his fingers out of me. I turned towards him with a look of protest.

"Jake?"

"This is 'Where Dreams Come True'."

"And get crushed too?" I stuck my tongue out at Jake. "Oooh, *puppy*!" I said cheerfully. "This is my favorite part!"

I loved the mangy dog that taunted the pirates with the key. It was a slight distraction from the release I really craved. My pussy was aching and wanted more. When we moved into the final room filled with piles of jewels and gold, Jake put his hand up to my mouth.

"Here's your treasure."

He pushed his soaked fingers past my lips. I licked and sucked at them eagerly while I straightened my dress. As we pulled into the unloading area, he took his hand back. The boat stopped, but before we were given the "all clear" to exit, he gave me a kiss.

"Mmmmmm, you taste good," he said with a smile.

We exited the boat and walked back into the gift shop we had met in earlier. Jake locked his fingers into mine and pulled me along quickly through the shop. I thought he was taking me back to the curio cabinet with the sinking boats, but we walked past it and through an archway that led out of the store.

"The ride's not over."

We stopped a few feet past the archway as he opened a door.

"Companion restroom, please step inside."

I did as he instructed and heard the lock click behind us. He quickly pushed me to the wall with my hands pressed against it, stood behind me, and pulled back on my hips. He tossed the skirt of my dress up onto my back and slid his hand between my legs.

"I fucking love No-Panties in the Park Day. This has got to be Disney's best idea *ever*!"

I felt him reach up and grab both of my pigtails and pull me to arch back.

"As much as I'd love to take my time, I've been wanting this for months and I'm not waiting one minute longer."

Sometimes an all-night sex marathon is what you *want*, but a quickie in a companion restroom is what you *need*. Jake's shorts fell to the floor and his cock slid between my legs. It was thick but I was still so soaked from his teases that the tip easily slid inside me. There were no more teases. He gave another tug on my pigtails and plunged deeply into me. His thrusts came hard and fast. It wasn't long until we both bit at our lips to stop from moaning and scandalizing the tourists.

Jake's moans turned to growls the more he pumped. I bounced my hips back wildly, riding his thick cock.

"I'll be your red-headed wench any time, Jake!" I moaned out.

Jake growled louder and slapped my ass. I felt him pulsing inside me, and felt cum running down my thigh. His strokes slowed and my orgasm came quickly. My pussy tightened around him and drained the rest of the cum from his shaft.

Jake released my pigtails and leaned his glistening chest against my back. His strong arms wrapped around the front of me and held me tightly. We both needed that; it had been far too long of a wait. Once we caught our breath, we straightened our clothes and shared the sink to cool our faces down.

Jake looked at me with a sparkle in his eye, "The pigtails are just as handy as I imagined."

"I told you, Jake!"

"So, what would you like to do now?"

"Dole whip?"

"Yes! *Dole whip!*"

Wet
Typhoon Lagoon Water Park

TYPHOON TILLY
Let's Go Slurpin', Typhoon Lagoon Water Park

1/2 oz. Blue Curacao
1/2 oz. Melon Liquor
1/2 oz. Banana Liquor
1 oz. Malibu Coconut Rum
4 oz. Pina Colada Mix
Blend with Ice

RY NOT TO get too wet," he said while flashing a cute smile.

I lowered my sunglasses and looked right into his eyes. "I enjoy being wet."

The young Cast Member at the entrance to Typhoon Lagoon lowered his head. I could see a slight blush rise on his cheeks.

"Have a magical day, Ma'am."

"You too, sweetie."

I made my way up the path at the entrance of the water park. It was mid-afternoon and the clouds were starting to roll in. It was a typical Florida summer. I knew the park wouldn't be open much longer, but an hour was more than enough time for me to relax and enjoy some tropical down time.

I decided to take a walk through the lush paths that wound around the park. I especially loved the small overlook bridges and hidden corners. I wanted to explore and I didn't mind getting lost there.

As I reached the back of the park, I passed by the bottom of the monstrous slide, Humunga Kowabunga. It's the type with one of those massive drops straight down that causes your bathing suit bottom to wedge up your ass and your top to fly off. Needless to say, there are usually some guys hanging out at the bottom of the slide waiting for that to happen to some poor, unsuspecting girl. There's an overlook off to the side where I always expect to see one or two. There were always guys who were more interested in waiting for a glimpse of a topless girl than getting in the water themselves, and that day was no different.

Even at Disney World, I have a knack for finding the perverts! There were four guys in their mid-thirties holding their drinks and leaning over the bamboo and rope railing of the overlook at the bottom of the Humunga Kowabunga slide. As I walked past, one of them turned around to yell to his friend. His shirt had the design of a pair of mouse ears that I recognized. They were not your typical Disney-authorized mouse ears. They had an anarchy symbol on them and the shirt said DSoD. It made me smile; I knew it well.

I paused for a moment a few feet away from him. "Nice shirt, darlin'."

He looked down at his chest to check what he was wearing, then looked up and smiled back. "Thanks!"

"I love *The Dark Side of Disney*." I kissed my hand and blew the kiss to him before walking off.

"Dayyyyumm," I heard him mutter under his breath as I left.

I couldn't help but smile. I always enjoyed stumbling upon the drunken park perverts. They're a very fun crowd.

The rain seemed to be holding off, so I decided to head to the wave pool. Sometimes it got very crowded in there, but I liked to swim up to the deep end and ride the waves back when they came. Surprisingly, they were much easier to handle in the deep end than they were back in the shallows. Depending on where you stood, the waves were sometimes strong enough to knock you down when they broke in the shallow area. I learned that the hard way that day.

I entered into the wave pool on the right side of the beach. With so much cloud cover, a lot of people had already left for the day and most of the beach chairs were empty. I wasn't worried about the weather, though, because I knew that

Disney had a pretty amazing weather watch system. If there was lightning in the area, lifeguards cleared everyone out fast. The Weather Channel had nothing on them for storm accuracy.

The water splashed up on my feet and ankles as I walked in, and it felt so nice and warm. I paused for a moment when I was in up to my knees. The waves had a really strong pull that could catch you off-guard. I made my way up to the right side, near the caution line in the water. Since it was nearly empty, I didn't feel the need to go to the deep area to avoid the typical elbow-to-elbow crowd. At that time, the waves were set to a pattern of just a mild bobbing effect and I happily bobbed along with them. After a few minutes of this, I couldn't stop thinking how helpful the motion would be for fucking. I looked around and saw there were lifeguards standing up on the high ledges near the deep end of the pool. There were also some scattered in the water to keep an eye on Guests in the moderate depth and shallows. So even if I brought my regular fuck buddy Cast Member friend, Jake, here some time, we wouldn't have enough privacy to take advantage of the "motion of the ocean".

Regardless of the reality of the situation, I couldn't help but fantasize about straddling Jake's lap and tightly wrapping my arms around his neck as we slowly fucked with the waves pushing us together. I was totally lost in my daydream when a strong wave crashed into me and pushed me off of my feet sideways and submerged me under the water. I flailed around, trying to stand up, but I was knocked into someone else's legs. Just as I tried to steady myself, a pair of strong hands grabbed hold of me under my arms and lifted me up above the water.

As my body came up from the water, the top of my bathing suit went down! I looked up at the man holding me by the arms as I stood in the water, topless in front of him. He just stared straight at my chest with his jaw dropped. He was one of the young lifeguards who I had seen standing in the water.

It was an awkward moment to say the least. I figured he had had enough of a peek so I pulled my top up to cover myself. I'm not usually shy, but after falling over and crashing into him, I wasn't exactly feeling sexy.

"Thank you," I said.

He didn't respond. He reached out and grabbed hold of me, hugging me to him.

I gasped but then suddenly felt the force of another wave hit me in the back and push me tighter into him. I held onto him closely. He felt so strong. I was starting to think it was definitely worth getting knocked over by a wave and looking like an idiot for this.

The wave passed and he said in a distinctly southern drawl, "You okay, Ma'am?"

I kept my arms locked around him and nodded.

"Maybe you'll be safer over there?"

He held onto me and guided me over to the right side of the pool near the wall.

He explained, "When the waves come, they can't come around that corner too darn well. They'll go past you about two feet away and the water next to the wall will stay mostly calm."

"Thank you very much... umm?"

"Travis, Ma'am." He let go of me and pulled up his lanyard with a name tag.

"Thank you, Travis."

"Awww it ain't nothin', Ma'am. You just stay safe and have a magical day."

I leaned against the wall while still standing in waist-deep water; watching him walk back towards the center of the pool. He looked barely twenty years old, lean but muscular, and deeply tanned... absolutely delicious!

I was lost in my fantasies again when I heard a gravelly voice speak to me.

"Having fun?"

"Huh? What?"

"Having fun?" he said.

In front of me was a tall man, a park Guest. He was trying to strike up a conversation. He looked to be in his mid-forties, balding, with a beer gut and a creepy, overgrown, porn mustache. Worst of all, he moved in front of me and was blocking my view of that delicious piece of bronzed meat, Travis.

"Yes, yes, I'm having a good time, thank you," I responded in a distracted tone.

He started to smile. "You know, I uh, I saw you take a little tumble there in the water. I just wanted to let you know that, umm, if you need some help with the, umm, ya know?" He put his hands up in front of himself and moved them up and down as if he was bouncing a pair of invisible tits, "Well, I'm here to help if you need anything."

Thankfully I was wearing sunglasses, or he would have seen me roll my eyes in disgust.

I nodded. "Thanks, but I think I'm fine."

He moved in a step closer to me and smiled even bigger. I stayed with my back against the wall, as far away from him as possible.

He opened his mouth slightly and licked his lips. "No, really, I'm here to heeellp."

Just as he was finishing his sentence, a wave came by and knocked him sideways off his feet. I started to laugh but then took the opportunity while he was under the water to exit the wave pool as quickly as possible. I didn't even look back, but I secretly hoped that Travis wouldn't bother to help pick him out of the water.

I stayed close to the side and turned left so that I only had to go a few steps through the beach until I was on the main path that led around the park. I knew there was an entrance to the lazy river not too far away, so if Mr. Creeper tried to follow me, I'd be long gone floating away.

I found the river entrance closest to me and grabbed an inner tube. I sat down into it while I was still standing on the submerged steps getting into the water. It only took a second to get situated before I pushed off the side and floated away to freedom.

I leaned back on my inner tube and stretched out. Again, nobody was around. The skies were still dark. At one point on my journey in the river, I felt a ray of sun kiss my cheek. It peeked in through the tree cover, but then was gone as quickly as it had come. I knew that the loop around the entire lazy river took half an hour, and I began to wonder if it had been a good idea to get in. The darker clouds started to roll in and I didn't want to be forced to exit the river on the opposite side of the water park from the entrance gate. Getting back to the car from there would not be fun in the midst of a tropical downpour with lightning. I decided not to worry too much about it. After all, I was already all wet.

As I circled the park on the river, I could tell that it was now almost completely empty. I was already more than halfway around but I only saw three people, and they were exiting. Each of the river entrances that I passed had piles of inner tubes blocking the stairs. Nobody was coming in or going out. I actually thought that maybe I had missed the announcement to clear the park for the storm. Had I been off in another daydream, I would have worried.

I kicked my toes up and trailed my fingertips in the water as my inner tube drifted along and slowly turned in circles. I knew that soon I would be up to my favorite part: the waterfall and cave. Each time I enjoyed the lazy river, I always made sure to stay in long enough to go under the waterfall and through the cave. Sometimes I would even circle again to go through twice. It was only a small section of the trip, but I always found it to be "mysterious" inside.

As my inner tube floated around the corner I saw the waterfall and cave entrance ahead, and I got excited. Then I noticed a long, lean, young man walking out from the side of the cave up on the land. He was wearing red lifeguard shorts. As I looked closer, I could make out the definition in his smooth, tanned abs. When my eyes finally moved up from his body to his face, I saw that it was that southern charmer, Travis. I knew that the lifeguards rotated positions often to keep sharp, but this was a nice surprise. He stopped on the bank of the lazy river, held his red floatation device casually down at his side, and rocked back and forth as he shifted his weight from one foot to the other. It was hard to tell if he was bored or swaying to a song in his own head.

Since nobody was around, I decided that I would put his skills to the test and relieve his boredom. About twenty feet from the cave entrance, right in front of where he was standing, I tipped my inner tube and screamed as I fell into the water. The water is not deep at all, but I still waved my arms and dramatically yelled for help. Even if he knew that I was faking my distress, he wasn't allowed to just let a screaming Guest drift away.

I actually expected him to toss in the big, red, floatation device that he held. Instead, he threw it aside and jumped in after me. He quickly took hold of my arm, and, before he could do much more, I clasped my arms around his neck and wrapped my legs around his hips, clinging to him and gasping for air. I could actually feel his belly shake a bit as he laughed at my obviously faked drowning panic. He put his arms around me in a hug and moved along towards the waterfall with our bodies still waist deep in the water.

I pulled my head back and looked at him. "Thank you again, Travis. You're my hero."

"You're welcome again, Ma'am."

Suddenly, we were both being pelted over the head with water! He carried me directly under the heaviest part of the water fall! I let go of him and turned away coughing with a mouth full of water. Obviously, he was trying to teach me a lesson for fake drowning, and he was successful.

As I made it to the side wall inside the cave, he grabbed hold of me and turned me around to face him again.

"We may have to get you some water wings if you keep having these problems, Ma'am. Guest safety always comes first." He winked as he gripped on to me tighter, and we continued to slowly float through the cave.

"Thank you for your concern, but I think that I'll be fine without those, Travis."

I put my hands against his chest and playfully pushed at him. He quickly pinned my back to the side wall near the exit of the cave and stopped us both from moving further with the current.

He whispered, "Ma'am, it would be in your best interest if you let me move you along to a location where you may safely exit the river. Your cooperation would be appreciated."

He pressed his body against me tightly and I could feel the rough surface of the faux rocks behind me digging into my skin. I ran my hands up over the front of his chest and looked into his eyes. He slowly moved his face in towards mine. I slid my hands from his chest up to his head and twirled my fingers around in his short hair.

I whispered back, "Yes, I understand. I'll do whatever you need to ensure my safety."

His lips pressed to me. His tongue teased its way between my lips and met mine. I was right. He definitely *was* delicious.

He pulled back from the kiss. I wanted more, but he turned away from me and reached out for an inner tube that was floating by.

He dropped the tube down over my head. "Just stay in there and I'll take you to a safe place, Ma'am."

I put my arms over the top of the inner tube and let my legs dangle down through the center into the water. I was perfectly capable of swimming, floating, or basically walking to the next exit, but what fun would that have been? I enjoyed the personal escort.

Travis held onto the handle on the side of the inner tube and I let him guide it. At a slow float, the next exit was about three minutes away. It was the same one that I entered from and was my planned exit location, anyway. The skies were getting very dark and I even felt a few sprinkles as we left the covering of the cave.

We floated along for nearly a minute without saying anything. I still felt my body trembling a bit from his unexpected kiss. I knew that others could see us and I didn't want to do anything that jeopardized his job. I just hoped that he would come home with me that night so we could continue where we left off in the cave.

As I plotted ways to convince him to come home with me, I felt his hand slide up my thigh in the water. I turned my head quickly and looked at him, surprised.

"Don't worry, Ma'am. I'll take care of you."

I let out a light sigh and put one foot down on the bottom of the lazy river to help me resist the current and gain more time with him. One of his hands remained on the top of the inner tube, guiding it as he walked along beside me. His other hand was under the water and between the back of my thighs. He pushed my bathing suit over with his fingertip and then slid the tip inside me. I closed my eyes and rested my face down onto the inner tube.

He continued playing with me. It made me wish that I had faked drowning on one of my trips there sooner. I felt the tips of two of his fingers working to push my pussy lips apart. He rubbed gently along them, teasing them open. Both fingertips then made their way inside. He held them steady then pulled them out a bit and slid them in deeper. I let out a faint moan and pressed my mouth down into the inner tube. Again, he slid them out and then pushed back in deeper yet, turning his fingers slightly to work them into me.

"You're almost there, Ma'am."

"Yessss," I moaned into the inner tube. "I'm almost there."

"Hey, Travis?!" a voice shouted from about forty feet in front of us. "Lightning. Park's closed. Can you check the shark reef?"

"Yeah, I got it!" Travis yelled back while slowly removing his fingers from my aching pussy.

We were coming up to the next river exit. I had no choice but to get out due to the lightning and park closing orders.

"Well, fuck," I mumbled as I looked at Travis.

He smiled back at me and laughed. I wanted to tear his shorts off and fuck him unconscious.

"You are a very naughty boy, Travis."

"Yes, Ma'am," he said proudly. "But I always make sure that every Guest is satisfied and has a magical experience before leaving the park."

"The park is closed, Travis. How do you plan on doing that? I'm not exactly feeling magical at the moment. Frustrated? Yes! Magical? Not so much!"

He pulled the inner tube off of me and tossed it up on the ledge. He took my hand as we walked up the stairs out of the lazy river. Instead of heading towards the front entrance of the park so that I could leave, he took my hand and escorted me in the opposite direction towards the shark reef snorkeling area.

The rain started to come down harder. We hurried back past the bathrooms and the huge shark jaws that adorned the entrance to the area. There were two small salt water tanks there that held several different types of fish including stingrays and sharks where Guests could float through the water with the fish. It was a small area, but still one of my favorite things to do at the park. In between the two salt water snorkeling tanks was a big, capsized ship. Basically, it was an underwater viewing area. If you went inside, you could see the fish and the Guests swimming by.

Travis led me down a ramp into the ship. The entrance was made from wide, wooden boards "haphazardly" nailed together. The ceiling and walls were made to look like they were collapsing. The inside of the ship was barren. It had a low ceiling and bare cement floor to simulate the abandoned wreckage of a ship. There were some metal rails in the ceiling that seemed to be used for storage, but that was it.

I was completely alone with Travis. The floor was wet from both the Guests trailing in water, and the hard rain making its way in through an open staircase on the other end of the hull. Travis left me standing in the middle of the room while he roped off the stairs. As he came back towards me, he took hold of me, tilted me back, and gave me another kiss. His lips were so soft, and they seduced me instantly. He really turned on the southern boy charm.

"Wait here, Ma'am. I'll be right back."

Travis left through the ramp where we came in and set up a Do Not Enter barrier cone in front of it. I could hear the rain coming down harder and beating onto the outside of the metal hull. I looked around the empty, eerie, room. Standing there all alone, I applauded the Imagineers for nailing the "abandoned shipwreck" feeling. I actually started feeling creeped out, so I went over to one of the portholes and looked through to see the fish. I wanted to relax. The water was cloudy and I couldn't see much. A few fish went by, but I struggled trying to get a glimpse of the sharks.

"Can I help you, Ma'am?"

I jolted up, startled. It was Travis walking back into the room!

"You scared me!"

He slowly strutted towards me. Even though he wore swim shorts, he walked like he was in cowboy boots. Just by the way he moved, I could see that he was very cocky for such a young man.

"I didn't mean no harm, Ma'am. Forgive me?"

He stood in front of me looking down. He had a devilish smirk. He reached around to the back of my neck and pulled the bow on my bathing suit. The straps instantly untied and my bathing suit top slid down. He gently wrapped his fingers around my throat, encouraging me to lean my head back. I closed my eyes in utter bliss from his sensual touch. This young creature was toying with me, and I loved it.

His hand released my throat and his palm flattened against my chest. He slowly slid it down until he was cupping my breast.

"Mmmmmm," I moaned.

Even my slight sound echoed inside the empty shell of the ship.

"You are very cocky for such a young man."

He smiled down at me again and lowered his soft lips to my nipple. I put my hands in his hair and pressed the back of his head gently onto my breast. He eagerly sucked at my nipple as his tongue twirled around, teasing me even more. My toes curled as his teeth lightly bit down and his tongue flicked.

"Fuck, you're such a good boy." My words echoed again through the room.

He stood up and spun me around by the shoulders so that I faced the portholes. He dropped to his knees, yanked the crotch of my bathing suit to the side, and plunged his face into my pussy from behind. I arched my back and spread my legs wide, inviting him in. His hands alternated between massaging up and down my hips and tightly gripping down into my flesh. His soft, wet, tongue pressed its way into me. I felt a flush of pure pleasure run over my body.

"You better fuck me soon, cowboy," I growled, with my face resting against the glass of the porthole.

He stood up and leaned forward over me. He covered my body with his and wrapped his arms around to firmly grip onto my breasts. I could feel his hard bulge pressing against my exposed pussy as he kept me bent forward. He slowly rotated his hips to rub against me.

"Is this what you want?" he asked.

He was too fucking sexy for his own good. I was not in the mood to continue being teased. I pushed back causing him to stand back up and I turned around to face him.

"*Yes!*" My scream echoed loudly through the room and startled me.

"Come get it."

He stepped a few feet to the side and I followed. We were standing under some metal rails that were bolted to the ceiling and wall. They curved out from the wall and seemed to be a resting place for some barrels. I had never paid much attention to the themed accessories along the ceiling before now.

Travis stood under the rails, facing me, and reached his arms up to grip onto them. He did a pull-up and in the same motion, reached out his legs towards me. His legs quickly wrapped around me. His ankles crossed over and hooked behind my back, pulling me to him and forcing my face to his crotch.

I gripped onto his hips to steady myself. I certainly wasn't expecting any gymnastics. His hard abs were right in front of my eyes. They were tan and ripped with lean muscles. He was cocky, but he had every right to be.

I ran my hands up onto his smooth tanned chest, mesmerized. He didn't wait for me to soak in the view. His hips rocked and pressed up towards my mouth. He was not at all subtle with what he wanted.

I wasted no time pulling his shorts down and releasing his cock. It was just as beautiful as he was. Just as smooth. Just as hard. Just as tan.

"Someone likes to be outside naked a lot. No tan lines?" I wrapped my hand around his hardness and slowly stroked him.

"Put it in your mouth. I wanna feel those lips," he said as he swung his body up again, rubbing his cock across my face.

"You forgot the 'Ma'am'."

"Suck my dick, Ma'am."

"Much better!"

I opened my mouth and slid my hands back to grip his ass. He slowly swung himself from the rails more, back and forth, back and forth. Each time, his cock slid into my waiting, wet mouth. As I suspected, his cock was just as delicious as the rest of him. I eagerly lapped at it each time it penetrated my lips.

I thought to myself, *"Swinging blow job while hanging from ceiling rails? And people wonder why I enjoy playing with young guys?"*

Just as I was finding my rhythm, he pulled his cock out of my mouth and released his legs, lowering himself to the floor. He pulled me to him and passionately engulfed my mouth with his.

As he continued to explore my mouth with his tongue, he guided me to the floor with him. It was rough and wet and dirty. But, I was in the mood for something rough, wet, and dirty! I expected that he was going to have my legs in the air in a matter of seconds, but he released me from the kiss and rolled onto his back.

He laid there naked, stroking his cock, and smiling at me. "Wanna go for a ride?"

"Yee-haw, cowboy!"

I stood up and lowered myself down over him, straddling his body with my ass towards his face. His throbbing dick slid right in to the hilt and I wasted no time riding him hard.

"Found me a cowgirl! Giddyup!" Travis slapped me on the ass and grabbed hold of my hips on both sides.

I bounced on his dick and he gripped tighter. He let me ride him at my own pace for a moment before he grabbed my arms, causing me to arch backwards and spread my legs wider. He lifted up his hips and took full advantage of the new position to pound my pussy deeper and harder.

"Oh *fuck*! Oh *fuck*! Oh *fuck*!" My screams echoed back and forth against the walls.

He reached up and took hold of my long hair and held them like reigns and slapped my bouncing ass again.

"Fuck, this is a beautiful view!" he said.

My back arched more and I leaned back towards his chest. His hips increased speed and thrust harder.

I screamed out, "*I'm gonna cum! Oh, please*! Come on baby. Fuck me. Fuck me!"

I felt his warm cum start pumping into me and I couldn't take anymore. I squirted all over his dick, drenching him and the cold, filthy, floor we were fucking on.

I collapsed back onto him, gasping for breath. He wrapped his strong arms up around me. His cock was still pulsing, but he was slowly calming down and sliding out of me.

He whispered in my ear, "You are much better on land than sea, Ma'am."

I responded, "I guess I'll have to fuck you in the bobbing wave pool sometime to debunk that theory!"

The Birthday Present
The Great Movie Ride

DIVA
Hollywood Brown Derby, Hollywood Studios

1 1/2 oz. Stoli Vanilla Vodka
1 oz. Godiva Chocolate Liquor
1 oz. Frangelico Hazelnut Liquor
Serve in a Chocolate Swirled Martini Glass

ALBERTO DANTE'S MILLIONAIRE CAPPUCCINO
Hollywood Brown Derby, Hollywood Studios

Hot Cappuccino
1/2 oz. Bailey's Irish Cream
1/2 oz. Grand Marnier
1/2 oz. Kahlua
1/2 oz. Frangelico Hazelnut Liquor
Top with Cappuccino Foam

iving so close to the Walt Disney World Resort provided me with the luxury of visiting the parks as often as I liked. I always took advantage of this fact. If I had a free day, I most likely went there, ordered a cocktail, and chatted up the Cast Members and Guests. That was my idea of a perfectly relaxing day. I simply loved the atmosphere, and I met some of the most friendly people that way. Many of them became my closest friends; our love of Disney added an extra element to our friendship. It bonded us.

I had met Jake in Hollywood Studios. He was working as a Cast Member there during *Star Wars* Weekends. It was months until we finally went on a date. The mind-blowing sex was worth the wait!

Jake was as adventurous as he was handsome. We saw each other regularly after our first date. I was nearly double his age, but it didn't seem to matter. He liked cougars, and I enjoyed his eager willingness to experiment. After a few dates, Jake introduced me to Holly and Bryn. They were all in the Disney College Program together and they all worked in Hollywood Studios. Jake took me to a few of their parties, where I learned that they were all up for damn near anything. I admired their free spirits. Some of my friends who were my age fell into a rut of being overly busy with life and forgot how to enjoy themselves like that.

The week of Jake's birthday, I decided to plan a special surprise for him. I talked to Holly and Bryn for suggestions. We didn't have to think too long to figure out what a twenty-four year-old guy wanted most for his birthday present. I could hardly contain my excitement when I called him to set up our date.

"Hey, Jake. How's my birthday boy doing? Excited for tomorrow yet?"

"I'm working tomorrow. Can I meet you in Hollywood Studios after I get off? At least we'll have the evening together. Just tell me where."

"That's perfect! I talked to Holly and Bryn about your birthday. They're working, too. They're closing at The Great Movie Ride. We can see them, then all go out together to celebrate. I haven't gone on that attraction in so long. Wanna go for a ride?"

"Definitely! I will *never* say 'no' to that question from you. Now I'm distracted thinking about it."

"Happy Birthday."

"Birthday bonus that we can hang with Holly and Bryn. You know how much they love it when I harass them at work."

"I'm sure they appreciate it, Jake. It's a shame that attraction is always so dead. But, you are a great cure for boredom. All the tourists will be at *Fantasmic!* at the end of the night. It will be a ghost town by then. We might as well enjoy the ride. Sound good?"

"The three of you together sounds *great*! You aren't plotting anything are you? Say yes! Please say yes!"

"Plotting? Do you really think that three, sweet, Disney-loving girls would plot something evil on your birthday? I'm hurt that you would think that, Jake."

"You're just fucking teasing me now. I know how you are. You wear a tiara, but it's held up by your horns!"

"I thought you enjoyed when I teased you?"

"You have *no* idea! I'll see you tomorrow, you sexy, evil,

princess."

"Sweet dreams, Jake."

When I arrived at Hollywood Studios, I took my time strolling down Hollywood Boulevard. I enjoyed looking at the nostalgic shop designs and how they contrasted with the frantic tourists. About halfway up the street, I stopped short. I was so excited to go see Jake that I almost ran the traffic light.

At the intersections along Hollywood Boulevard, there were several old-fashioned stop lights mounted into the sidewalks. All day long, they flipped signs back and forth from "Go" to "Stop." Each time they changed, they made a loud "*Bing*" sound. I always took notice of the signs and listened for the "*Bing*". If the sign said "Stop", I did. I did so, not because there was actually any real traffic or even a real road, but because *that* small detail pulled me into the magic. I respected it. A working sign wasn't necessary, but it was still there.

I stood still as the people rushed around me. Not a single other one of them noticed the sign. It was a shame. Most of them probably could have used a nice *stop* moment during their vacation. Again, I heard the sign go "*Bing*" and it changed from "Stop" to "Go".

I told Jake that I'd meet him under the Sorcerer's Hat: the big blue eyesore that blocked the view of the Chinese Theater. I often used it as a meet-up spot. It was the only good purpose I had ever found for it. I waited less than a minute before I heard his voice.

"Hey there, evil princess. Come here often?"

I turned around and saw Jake just a few feet away, walking towards me.

"Yes, yes I do. I'm a regular and expect some extra Cast Member magic."

"I'm at your service to make all of your dreams and wishes come true."

He pulled me close into one of his famous bear hugs. He smelled so good. He had a magical gift for knowing exactly how much cologne to wear to make me want to ravish him. I hugged him back tightly.

"Happy birthday, handsome."

"Thank you. I need a drink."

"Oh, one of those kinda days?"

"Yeah. I love my job. I love the Guests. But sometimes, I don't know what people are thinking. I make magic, not miracles!"

He released me from the hug. I ran my hands over his hard chest and up to his neck. I lightly massaged his neck and down his shoulders.

"Wow. You are tense. You really do need to relax."

We headed towards the new outdoor lounge at the Brown Derby restaurant. Behind a black iron fence, tables lined the patio next to the side exit door. They faced a path that connected Animation Courtyard to the corner of Hollywood and Vine. In the evening, the path filled with Guests hurrying towards the *Fantasmic!* theater and it became a great place to people watch.

When we arrived, the tables were all full. Luckily, a young couple motioned for us to take their table as they left. That was a relief since I had planned to meet-up with Holly and Bryn in about an hour. Our server arrived quickly, he handed us appetizer and cocktail menus then dashed away. Jake never looked at his menu. As soon as the server stepped away, he tugged on my chair and pulled us closer together.

"I missed my red-headed wench," he whispered into my ear.

He softly kissed my cheek, then my lips. His hand wandered onto my thigh and I felt my dress rise. I quickly slapped my hand onto his and held it from moving any farther.

"Hey! None of that, young man! There are people everywhere! Besides, I have a surprise for you later."

"I love your surprises! What is it?!" he said eagerly.

I ignored him. I pulled the menu up to cover my face and

block him out of my line of vision.

"Always the teasing princess."

The server returned to take our orders.

"I'll have the millionaire... something or other," said Jake.

I shifted my eyes from my menu to look at him and snickered.

"What? It's my birthday. I'm dreaming big."

I turned towards the server. "Surprise me."

He bowed slightly and nodded. "Yes, Princess," he said, and then walked away.

Jake raised an eyebrow and glared at the server as he left. He tugged my chair closer.

"How do you always do that?"

"Do what?"

"Get that response from men!"

"It's the tiara. It's the power of the sparkle. Embrace it. That's how I got you, my dear boy."

"Ohhhh yeah. The pigtails and big tits helped, too."

I stuck my tongue out at him. He laughed and slumped back into his seat, exhausted. Our drinks came out within a few minutes. Mine looked like milk. It was served in a martini glass lined with a swirl of chocolate syrup. It looked delicious.

"It's so pretty. It reminds me of a boozy milkshake."

"Be careful. The drinks are strong here."

I took a quick sip and instantly felt a burn slide down my throat. I swallowed and exhaled from the sensation.

"Wow. That is deceptive. It's just a glass of vodka in disguise!"

"I warned you. I should order you another," he teased.

I stuck my tongue out at him again and then took another sip.

"I don't think that will be necessary. I have a feeling you're gonna get lucky, anyway."

I reached towards him and stroked the back of my hand down his cheek. I guided his face by the chin to give me a kiss.

The taste of our cocktails mixed well on our tongues. I slid my hand under the table and up his inner thigh. A firm bulge was waiting for me.

"Feeling more relaxed, Jake?"

"Oh yeah. I'm ready to get this birthday started."

We finished our drinks and paid the check. *Fantasmic!* had started. The attractions were all about to close and we wandered towards The Great Movie Ride to catch the last ride of the night. I raised my hand to give the Sorcerer's Hat a quick one-finger salute as we passed near it.

"The Chinese Theater is a beautiful building. The Sorcerer's Hat frustrates me."

Jake pointed to the stage. "At least the Hat is blocked by the stage now."

"Yes, that's much better. What do you think they'll build next to block the stage that blocks the Hat that blocks the Theater?"

"Starbucks?"

"I'm okay with that. I need all the caffeine I can get to stay awake in this park now."

We walked through the Chinese Theater courtyard to enter the attraction. The Great Movie Ride was empty. We actually asked the Cast Member standing outside the entrance if it was still open and I was stunned when he nodded yes.

As we wound through the long queue inside the building, I told Jake about the first year that the ride opened.

"This place was a madhouse. That's why the line winds around so much inside here. They needed all this space for all the Guests who wanted to ride it. You know how Toy Story Mania is now?"

"Really?" he responded in disbelief.

"Yep! The line went the entire way through the interior, outside, through those covered areas off to the right of the main doors, and across the open patio on the side. I stood in it on many hot summer days."

We reached the final waiting area for the ride. It looked like a movie theater with rows of metal rails instead of seats. The far wall had a movie screen that played clips of classic movies. The room could have held a few hundred people but we were the only ones there. We walked back and forth through the pointless queue. Near the movie screen in the front of the room was a door that lead to the ride-car loading area. A teenage-looking Cast Member was leaning against the wall near the doorway. He looked like he might be asleep. Jake spoke up to alert him that we were there.

"Slow night?"

He opened his eyes and fumbled around, disoriented.

"Huh? Ummm. Yeah. I'm new, but I think it's always like this."

He directed us into the next room. A big ride-car was sitting there, empty. Nobody directed us to sit in any particular place, so we chose the second row directly behind where we knew our attraction tour guide stood.

All of a sudden, our guide popped up into the car. It was Holly!

"Hey guys! You made it!" she said in her typical extra perky way.

Holly was an adorable, petite, blonde, with a bobbed haircut and a bright smile. She was so cute and sweet. She was the embodiment of the ultimate Disney Cast Member. With her peppy attitude, I expected to see her working as Cinderella one day soon.

She leaned over the seat and gave us each a quick hug before starting her spiel. She performed like a pro. Although we were the only two there, she carried on as if the entire ride-car was full of Guests. We hadn't even left the loading area yet and we were already thoroughly entertained.

As we moved under the colorful glowing lights of the first scene, I could hear the music from *Singing in the Rain*.

"Jake, am I the only one who thinks of Stanley Kubrick's

A Clockwork Orange when I hear that song? Ultraviolence and sex. It's another iconic movie classic!"

Jake tilted his head at me. "That's totally fucked up."

I glanced to my right and saw Mary Poppins singing. From *A Clockwork Orange* to Mary was an awkward mental transition.

We moved into the gangster scene and I slipped my hand onto Jake's thigh and quickly ran it up to his crotch. He rose up in his seat, looking slightly embarrassed.

"Hey! Wait, is this my surprise?"

"Perhaps."

I started to unbutton his shorts. When I talked to Holly the day before, she told me that people had been doing some very naughty fun activities on the ride every night for the past week. I didn't know if there were budget cutbacks that reduced the monitoring of the attraction, or if this attraction just had such low attendance at night that nobody paid attention or cared. Regardless, "The Last Ride of the Night" had become legendary with the Cast Members who worked there. I was shocked that Jake didn't know about it yet since he worked in that park.

Our car stopped at the end of the gangster scene. A female gangster appeared from behind the set wielding a gun. It was Bryn! She wore a female version of a mobster pin-striped suit. The skirt was long and she couldn't even close the jacket properly. It looked funny on her because her huge boobs were trying to force their way out. There must have been some backstage mix-up. I had no idea how she ended up wearing that clearly unapproved costume.

Jake smiled at her as I slid my hand into his shorts. Bryn broke character for a second to smile back and wave "hi" with her gun.

In the few seconds that it took Bryn to "hijack" our car from Holly, I had Jake exposed and hard. Given the situation, it was not that difficult of a task.

"Move up into her seat," I said to Jake.

Jake looked puzzled.

"Go on."

He stood up and his shorts fell to the floor. I smacked his cute ass as he spun around, then he pulled his legs over the seat and slid down into the driver's seat of the vehicle. Bryn stood in the small space in front of him with her tits a few inches from his face. She never missed a line from her script.

I leaned forward and ran my hands through the back of Jake's hair.

"Lift her skirt, darlin'. Your birthday present is waiting."

Bryn kept talking into the microphone in her horrible Cagney-like gangster accent while Jake lifted her skirt. She was pantiless and shaven bare.

"Well, look at that Jake. I never looked at the Parks Times Guide for today. It must be No Panties in the Park Day for the Studios."

"I fuckin' love No Panties in the Park Day!" he said.

Bryn looked down at Jake. "Enjoy it birthday boy. You've got four and a half minutes."

She shoved Jake's face into her crotch and held it there tightly.

"Mind your P's and Q's and nobody gets hurt."

Bryn's gangster accent was horrible but funny. It didn't improve much as Jake eagerly lapped at her pussy. She ground down onto his face while we slowly moved through the western scene. She held up the microphone and continued reciting the script. Her voice became robotic as she struggled to say the words.

We moved into the next scene. An automated recording described the film, *Alien*. Jake pulled his head back.

"I hate this room!"

Bryn barely allowed him to finish his sentence before she shoved his face back into her crotch. He wrapped his hands around her ass and gripped his fingers down in to her flesh. I could see Bryn's chest rise and fall rapidly. I leaned in over the seat and encouraged Jake.

"You love having that warm, wet pussy rubbing all over your face don't you? If you make her cum really hard, maybe she will give you another birthday treat."

I could hear Jake moan as he nodded his head up and down in agreement while it was still buried between Bryn's legs. Bryn rose up on to the tips of her toes as she moaned. Jake moved his hand between her legs to finger her pussy. His mouth broke free from her clit just long enough to spread her wet lips apart and slide two fingers deep inside her. His tongue returned to her clit. Then just as we passed under the screeching ceiling alien, Bryn screeched too. Jake pumped his fingers, sucked on her clit, and forced her to cum all over his face and hand. Her head fell back and I could see her body trembling as she panted, trying to catch her breath.

She pushed Jake's head away. Within a few seconds, she dropped down onto her knees in the small space between Jake's legs and happily returned the favor. She held onto her microphone and broke away from Jake as needed to continue her script. I admired her dedication to properly do her job while she continued to suck cock.

We moved out of the *Alien* room and I couldn't help but laugh when I heard her voice continue the next line in the script: "That's enough creepy crawly things for one day."

As the car entered the *Indiana Jones* room, Jake put his arms into the air like he was on a roller coaster. While Bryn sucked his cock he sang along with the Indiana Jones theme music... *very* loudly, "Da... Da... Da... Daaaa... Da... Da... Daaaa."

Bryn's mumbled monotone voice rang out from the speakers while she stayed curled up on the floor. "Snakes, why'd it have to be snakes?"

Jake's arms dropped quickly when he heard her, and I nearly fell off the seat from laughing so hard.

The next room of the attraction was designed to look like

a temple. Bryn was required to exit the car and climb up the temple to switch places with Holly. We stopped, and Bryn stood up from between Jake's legs. His head fell back against the seat. I saw his chest heaving as he took in deep breaths and attempted to recover. I sat on the edge of the seat behind him and ran my hands down over his chest. He moaned as I kissed along his neck.

"Having fun, birthday boy?"

"This is so fucked up! It's the best birthday ever!"

"There's still more. Move back here with me. I wanna play, too."

Jake jumped up and I saw his dick was bulging at the seams. I knew he was ready to cum.

We kissed and fondled each other like teenagers in the backseat of a car. His hands explored under my dress. I stroked his well-sucked dick. We clawed at each other. We hardly noticed when Holly returned as our tour guide until the ride-car started to move again.

Holly continued doing her squeaky, bubbly, overacted, spiel. She and Bryn were flawless in their ability to mix work and play.

We entered into the Fantasia room. Cold bursts of air whipped around us and blew through my hair. I opened my eyes and saw Mickey Mouse dressed as the Sorcerer's Apprentice. Animation of Mickey played on the wall next to us. I instinctively pushed at Jake's hands to stop him from touching me.

"No, no, stop!"

"What? Why?" he growled.

I pointed up to the screen to the left. "Mickey is watching. It's just not right."

Surprisingly, Jake nodded in agreement and placed his hand on his lap. Our anticipation was overwhelming as we both attempted to sit there patiently for the few seconds it took to move out of the room.

We approached the very brightly lit *Wizard of Oz* scene and I quickly leaned over and plunged my mouth down over Jake's cock. The munchkins popped their heads out of all the cute little houses and sang *Ding Dong! The Witch is Dead!*

Jake's head fell back and I heard him moan, "This is *sooo* fucked up!"

I laughed at his reaction. He grabbed the back of my head and held my hair as my throat vibrated around the head of his cock. I expected his warm cum to fill my mouth any second.

Suddenly, the Wicked Witch popped up in a puff of smoke in front of us. Jake freaked out and pulled at my hair to lift my head up.

"No, no, no! Stop!" he yelled.

"What the fuck, Jake?!"

"I can't cum with the Wicked Witch right there! I don't want that on my resume!"

I burst out into laughter. I was tempted to put my mouth back around his cock and force him to cum, but I decided to be nice on his birthday.

After perky Holly scared off the witch, Jake grabbed me by the hair and pushed my face back down over him. The munchkins all returned to serenade us again. I hummed along with them to the tune of *Follow the Yellow Brick Road*.

Jake's body clenched up. I felt his balls tighten, but he fought off his explosion while the music blared.

"Munchkins. Mother fucker! This is *so* fucked up!"

We moved into the last room of the attraction and our ride-car parked in front of a large movie screen. It was very dark except for the light from the screen. Holly finished her spiel before the movie clips montage began and then she climbed over the seat and onto the other side of Jake.

"We have less than three minutes 'til I have to jump back!"

"Not gonna be a problem," Jake assured her.

We took turns sucking his cock and touching all over his body. As Holly trailed the tip of her tongue around the head of Jake's dick, I nibbled on his inner thigh. When I put my mouth to his balls, I felt them tighten so I slowly dragged my tongue up the length of his shaft towards Holly's busy tongue. Our mouths met and our tongues tangled around his cock together. None of us watched the screen, but Holly giggled when we heard Robin Williams scream, "*Gooood Mornin' Vietnam!*"

Jake mumbled again. "Sooooo fucked up."

The film was almost over. Holly and I fought over Jake's cock with our mouths. We both had our tongues on his dick as the *Star Wars* theme music began to play. Jake let out a low, deep, moan as cum shot up and covered both of our faces. He placed his hands on the backs of our heads then pressed our mouths together. We licked the cum off of each other and slowly kissed while our heads rested in his lap.

Holly couldn't linger too long. Before the movie ended, she stood up, jumped back over the seat, and grabbed her microphone. Our ride-car started to move again. She thanked us for joining her on the ride and instructed us on how to make a dramatic Hollywood exit. Her arms waved around as she spoke in her typical, energetic, Holly fashion. Her face still glistened with the aftermath of wetness from our kisses and Jake's cum.

"...and when I yell action, don't forget the thunderous applause for yours truly. Aaaanddd, *Action!*"

I clapped. Jake hooted, screamed, clapped, and whistled like his favorite team had just won the Superbowl! Holly curtseyed and blushed as if she had just received an Academy Award. We exited the ride and made our way to the door. The new Cast Member who was asleep when we arrived commented to us.

"Did you enjoy the ride?"

"Yeah!" said Jake. "Love the new upgrades!"

"Great! Thanks!" said the young man. "Wait, huh?"

We walked out of the building into an empty park, one-finger saluted the Sorcerer's Hat again, and headed down Hollywood Boulevard towards the parking lot.

"So, did you like your birthday present Jake?"

"Definitely! Three-girl blow jobs are *always* the perfect gift."

As we took our time strolling down the street, Jake couldn't stop talking about how much fun he had with his birthday surprise. Aside from his voice, the park was quiet.

Bing!

I grabbed Jake's arm and held him. "Stop!"

Jake gave me a puzzled look. I pointed up at the "Stop" light on the sidewalk. We stood there in an empty park, waiting silently.

Bing!

The sign changed to "Go". I started to walk towards the exit. Jake stayed still.

"You coming, Jake?"

He put his head down, shook it slightly in bewilderment, and walked towards me. I heard him mutter:

"So fucked up."

Come Here Little Boy
Saratoga Springs Resort

STRAWBERRY MINT JULEP
Resort Shared Drink Menu

1 Large Strawberry, Muddled
6 Mint Leaves, Muddled
1 oz. Agave Nectar
1 oz. Fresh Lemon Juice
2 oz. Maker's Mark Bourbon
Serve Over Ice

I MET ADAM IN St. Augustine shortly after moving to Florida. He was a young guy in his late twenties. I was much older than him, almost twelve years (hey, embrace the cougar years right?). He was really tall, at least 6' 4". He was also very toned, but thin, and he had tattoos on his arms and calves. The best one was across his back from shoulder to shoulder. It looked like a tribal design. I didn't know what it was supposed to be, but it sure did make for a nice view laying in bed next to me in the morning. He had mesmerizing bright blue eyes and freckles. He was a ginger. I had never played with a ginger before.

Adam and I talked on the phone and texted a lot before we had our first date. I adored flirting with him, and eventually we met for coffee. I had a moment of wanting to corrupt him, but I learned quickly that those days had probably passed. He had been in the Army for eight years prior to starting college and had experienced a lot on his tours around the world. Now he was out of the military and finishing his junior year.

Adam finished his finals the day before our first date. I became excited when he told me that he just completed a Psychology of Disney class. I had no idea such a thing existed, let alone how many books were written on the subject. From his description, it seemed that a "Disney" college class wasn't as easy as he expected. He was frustrated by how difficult it was. Part of his lure to convince me to join him for coffee was that he offered me all of his class books. He didn't want to ever look at them again, and he knew that he couldn't get much money trying to resell them. I couldn't resist. One man's trash is another crazy Disney princess' treasure! Disney, books, coffee, and a hot young Army boy seemed like the perfect date to me.

As we talked over coffee, I mentioned that my birthday was in a week and that I was headed to Disney World for a quick overnight trip. Adam had a very bold personality: halfway through our date, he invited himself along on my trip. I tried to explain to him that I had other plans. I didn't give him the details, but I had recently met a young, handsome, Cast Member, Jake, during *Star Wars* Weekends at Hollywood Studios. He'd slipped me his number and a couple of free *Star Wars* collectibles. I really wanted to spend some time with him and get to know him better. I expected me and Jake to have a lot of fun at the parks together while he was there on the College Program. However, I decided to explore my curiosity about the tall Army boy and let the Cast Member meet-up slide for the time being.

The day came for my birthday trip and I told Adam that I was driving over to Disney World in the afternoon. I explained that I wanted to relax before having company, so he would have to wait until later in the evening before he could join me at my hotel. But, as I was driving, he texted that he was already on his way there. I was slightly irritated but flattered at the same time. I liked that he was so eager to see me. However, after he invited himself on the trip, I was not pleased that he decided to invade the quiet time that I wanted as well. He was lucky that he was very handsome, or I would have told him to go back home.

I arrived on Disney property and checked in at Saratoga Springs. It was my first time at that particular resort and I was not excited about it. In fact, I had a friend who always called it Snoratoga Springs. I would have preferred to stay at the Beach Club, but it was the only room available on short notice. Check-in was uneventful. My room was ready. That was a happy start for my trip. I put on my free Birthday Celebration button that was given to me at check-in and headed to my studio villa.

I loved that delicious blast of air-conditioning that I got as I entered my room. A towel animal three-circle Mickey head decorated the bottom of the bed. I always appreciated those little Disney touches. I tossed my bag on the table, flopped down on the couch, and put my feet up. I closed my eyes. It felt good to be back on Disney soil.

Within a minute, my phone beeped. It was a text from Adam! He was already there! I was barely settled and he hadn't respected my request for some alone time on my birthday. So, I figured this was a good time for a little life lesson. His cute, young, ass needed to calm the fuck down.

I texted back to him, explaining *again* that I wanted some alone time and that I would let him know when I was ready for company. I instructed him to wait in his truck at the Carriage House check-in area. That was the consequence of his choice to ignore my wishes. I told him that I'd give him the room number when I wanted to see him.

I put my bathing suit on and walked to the pool for a relaxing soak. I realized that I loved the quiet pool near my building. It was along the edge of the lake and I could look out over it to see Downtown Disney. It was beautiful! I floated around enjoying the sun and thought about what the evening had in store. I must have had some special look in my eye because there were two young male Guests there who kept smiling at me. They looked delicious but I had to remind myself that I didn't have time for *all* the boys. At least not that night.

I noticed the sun beginning to lower in the sky. I was upset about not having enough time for Downtown Disney. I had planned for a good hour of birthday shopping that evening, but Adam was still waiting in his truck. He should *not* have arrived so early! It had been about an hour though, and I didn't want to be too cruel... yet.

I went back to my room, showered, and changed. I took pictures of myself as I did so and sent them to Adam as a glimpse into his future. First, a full-body pose, dripping wet, straight out of the shower with a towel draped in front of me. Next, a close up of my breasts peeking out from behind the black lace of my lingerie gown. Sometimes there's nothing more delightful than teasing an eager boy. I felt aroused and wet already, *until* he texted me that he had found my car in the parking lot and was sitting next to it. I had no idea how he had found me, he must have circled each section of the parking lot looking for my car. Saratoga Springs was a *massive* resort! I swear a man with a determined dick could do *anything* he set his mind to!

He begged over and over to come inside. I would have let him in sooner, but *again* he hadn't followed my simple requests! He moved his truck! I think the term "blue balls" was an understatement to describe his suffering. Yet each time he defied me, I cared less and less about his desires.

By this time, I was eager to play, too, but I took my time. After I was fully dressed, I set up the room with a few special surprises. During our coffee date, we had discovered that we had similar interests... similar *kinky* interests. So, I had brought along a little toy bag of pleasure. It was my birthday after all, and I wanted to celebrate. He had a lot of experience, but I knew that I could find something new to teach him.

In my studio room at Saratoga, there was one queen bed and a sofa bed. The coffee table in front of the sofa was a padded bench that had a wooden tray resting on top to serve as a table-top. The tray reminded me of something used to serve breakfast in bed. I opened my luggage and carefully laid out my toys. I filled the tray with all kinds of fun things that could be used to tease and torture overly-eager little boys. My favorite item was a paddle that a friend had handmade as a gift for my previous birthday. It was a thick piece of wood carved into the shape of a large crown with a handle on it. It was pink on one side and black on the other. Each side had words handwritten on it. The pink side said "Sweet Ass Princess". The black side said "Bad Ass Princess". It was my special birthday paddle.

I laughed to myself when I thought about the little boy's ass that was going to be taking my birthday spankings this year!

Once I was ready for him, I went over to the entrance door, opened it slightly, and flipped the security latch open. I rested the door closed on it so that it stayed cracked and unlocked. I walked across the room to the tray that held all of the toys. I reached down and curled my finger around a small chain. I pulled it up slowly. It was a five-foot long dog leash. I had modified it with a key ring part-way up the length so that the hook at the end would have something to latch onto and create its own makeshift collar.

Across from the sofa was a table with two chairs. I sat down at the chair closest to the window and placed the leash on the table. I picked up my phone from the table and called Adam.

"Hello? Can I come in now?" Adam eagerly asked.

"You should have the manners to say hello first, Adam."

"I...."

"Pay attention please. *This time do as I say*! The door is unlatched. Come in. Close and lock it behind you. There is a small nook at the entrance with a mirror and small shelf. Put your things in that area. Take off all your clothes. Then come over to me and kneel down in front of me. Understand?"

His voice cracked. "Yes, Princess."

"Up the path near my car. First room on the right. You'll see the unlatched door."

It was less than a minute before I heard the door slowly

open. I should have made him wait longer! I sat quietly while
he did what I told him... for once. I could hear his keys jingle
as he put them on the small shelf at the entrance. I heard him
kick his shoes off and heard the distinct sound of his zipper
opening. Suddenly, I felt like the one who was too eager to
wait.

He walked towards me. His tattooed arms and tall, thin,
swimmer's build looked so inviting. He had just enough bad
boy edge to look dangerous. He stared right through me as he
approached. He was already aroused, all ten inches of him. He
gave a slight smile that took me off-guard for a brief second.
I looked down at the floor and he knelt down in front of me.

"Hello, Adam."

"Hello, Princess," he responded softly. "Happy birthday."

"Thank you, pet. How are you?"

"Excited," he said quickly.

"Yes, I noticed. You need to learn patience for the future.
You should be glad that I'm nice. I was tempted to leave you
outside for another hour."

I leaned forward and kissed him gently on the forehead.
My large breasts brushed against his face. I trailed the kisses
down his cheek and to his neck, then up to his ear.

"Would you like to play with me?"

"Yessssss, Princess!"

I couldn't help but laugh at his reaction.

I leaned back on the chair, reached over to the table, and
picked up the leash. I held it in front of him, then gently
touched it to his lips so that he could feel the chill of the
metal. I circled his neck slowly with the chain and latched it to
the key ring. It had several inches of slack and draped loosely
from his neck.

"You look lovely in chain."

Adam lowered his eyes to the floor.

I placed my hand to his chin and raised his face up.

"Don't hide those pretty blue eyes from me, handsome."

I held onto the handle of the leash and twirled my hand around to gather up the loose chain. I stood up in front of him and lowered the top of my gown. I barely clear five feet tall, so his kneeling height put his face right in front of my breasts. I tugged the leash and pulled his face to my chest. He kissed and sucked at them eagerly. Too eagerly. I grabbed the back of his head and forced his face tighter to my chest. My tits were large enough to nearly bury his face. I could hear him trying to suck in air to breathe. It only made me hold him tighter. He squirmed around, but that just made me laugh. He was a strong boy. If he wanted free, he could have pushed me away. Instead, he put his arms around my hips and clung to me. He was right where he wanted to be.

I pushed him back from me, and he gasped for air. I didn't give him time to recover. I pulled at the leash again to keep him straight up on his knees.

"Tell me how much you enjoyed that." I nudged his rock hard cock with my foot. "Don't try to lie to me. This gives away all your secrets."

"Yes, Princess. I loved it. Thank you."

"Good boy! Now I have a reward for you. You know it's my birthday."

"Yes, Princess."

"I'm going to give you the honor of taking my birthday spankings. Would you like to do that for me, Adam?"

He eagerly nodded. I think he would have agreed to walk through fire at that moment if I told him to!

I leaned in and teased my lips across his. I reached down with my right hand and gripped tightly around his dick. He gasped and I took the opportunity to muffle him with a forceful kiss while stroking his dick for a few seconds. When I broke away from him, I actually saw his dick jump like it would follow me wherever I was going with or without him.

"Down. On all fours."

I gave the leash a slight tug and led him crawling towards

the sofa. I saw his eyes light up when he noticed the big tray of toys sitting there. I know we had discussed that he was kinky too. He certainly had been agreeable to everything so far, but I think he was still taken off-guard seeing my selection of playthings.

When he reached the sofa, I pushed his head to the seat while he stayed on his hands and knees.

"Stay right there."

I released the chain in my hand so that I was just holding the handle. The leash draped down along the side of his body. I had enough slack now to keep hold of him while I reached for what I needed. What I needed was my lovely princess paddle. I picked it up and bent over so that my face was next to his on the seat of the couch. I gave the leash another tug so he would look at me then I held the paddle up in front of his face.

"Lookie! It's made special for princesses!" I held the black side towards him. "See, it says 'Bad Ass Princess'!"

He nodded in agreement but didn't say anything. I think my giddy demeanor after I picked up the paddle gave him strong concern about how sadistic I would be if given the opportunity.

I twirled the paddle in my hand so that the pink side was showing.

"It has a pink side too! That's the 'Sweet Ass Princess' side! Don't you think I'm sweet?"

I quickly reached back and smacked him hard on his little bare ass. He jolted up.

"Don't you?" I repeated in a more demanding tone.

"Yes, Princess, yes!" he quickly replied.

"Awwww, did that hurt?" I laughed. "Well, I'm turning forty-one now. There's a lot more to go. So, you might want to get used to it!"

Again, I quickly reached back again and landed several hard slams onto his ass. He actually yelped!

"Oh come on," I said. "It's *pink* for fuck's sake! It can't hurt that much!"

I rested the paddle on the small of his back and reached down towards his dick. It still felt plenty hard to me. I teased my fingertips up and down over it and gave him a moment to relax after the startling smacks. Using one finger, I very lightly circled the head of his throbbing cock and felt the precum leaking from him. I leaned towards his neck and tasted him. He let out a soft sigh.

"Don't get too comfortable, pet."

I picked up the paddle again and landed a few more firm taps. He was getting very dark pink by this time so I rubbed his bottom gently and patted it sweetly with my hand. As I did this, he turned his head and looked over his shoulder at me with pleading, puppy dog eyes. It was then that I noticed the throw pillows on the sofa next to his head.

Saratoga Springs was an equestrian themed resort. There was horse stuff everywhere. Each pillow resting on the couch had the portrait of a horse from a Disney animated film. I didn't even know what films they were from. But they had distinctly human expressions. One of them looked a bit stunned and the other looked condescending. Both were rather smug!

They were *mood-killer pillows!*

I decided that they must have been some Imagineering joke to make sure nobody ever attempted to fuck in the resort's rooms. I momentarily stopped the birthday spanking torture and tugged his leash to relocate.

"Crawl towards the bed... *now!*"

I was irritated by the disruption in our play. He only needed to crawl a few feet to the bed, but I took the opportunity to paddle his ass the entire way. That quickly helped my mood.

"Rip all of the blankets off the bed."

I released the leash and he got up. He pulled the comforter and blanket off the bed but left on the sheets. I stood behind him and ran my hands all over his naked body; I couldn't help myself. I reached around to his cock and stroked it. My firm touch slowed his progress with the bed, but I wasn't in any hurry. His red ass needed a break, anyway.

After the bed was stripped and the blankets tossed onto the floor, I grabbed his leash again and pulled him closer to me.

"Kiss me."

He ran his hands up into my long hair, down my neck, and over my still-exposed breasts. Then his lips pressed firmly to mine. It almost took my breath away. I wanted him, but not just yet.

"Lay face down across the bottom of the bed."

There was no way his tall frame was fitting any direction in the bed without dangling off the end. He obeyed. His head went towards the wall that divided off the bathroom area. His feet were off the end towards the open room.

I ran my hand down over him. First, over his back and towards his ass, and then between his legs, forcing them apart a bit. As my hand slid down over his balls, I heard him moan even with his face pressed into the mattress. I grabbed the paddle again and held it against his ass. He clenched at the touch even without feeling the sting.

"Let's play good or evil. That seems like an appropriate game for a trip to Disney World. I'll give you a smack, and you tell me what color it was that hit you. The *good* sweet, pink side or the *evil* bad, black, dark, side. Okie dokie?"

I didn't give him a chance to agree before pulling back and landing another blow. He arched up off the bed and his toes curled.

"Good or evil, pumpkin? What ya think?"

"*Evil!*" he yelled out "*Evil!*"

"Are you sure?"

I hit him a half-dozen more times rapidly while he squirmed all around.

"*Yessss, evil... darkside!*"

I put the pink side in front of his face and leaned towards

him.

"Nope."

I reached back and smacked him a few more times with the pink side again. I really had no idea what number we were on for the birthday spankings. He probably should have thought about counting too, to literally save his ass.

"How was that? Good, or evil?"

"*Evilll!*"

I gave a tiny tug to his leash and he looked at me. I showed him the pink side again.

"You really aren't very good at this game."

I started to laugh.

"That's *it!*" he shouted.

"Huh?"

Before I knew it, he was up on his knees in front of me as I sat next to him on the bed. He put his hands on my shoulders and gave me a shove. I fell onto my back with my head landing at the top of the bed onto a pillow. My lace gown flew up, and the leash slipped out of my hand. He quickly pounced on top of me and pinned me down by the wrists. He looked down at me, smiling.

"You're such a teasing little princess."

I squirmed around under him but responded with only whimpers.

"Awww, where you trying to squirm off to, Princess?"

He leaned down and started kissing me hard while he pressed his throbbing cock against my thigh. I couldn't help it, my hips started rising up towards him... wanting him. He pulled away and lifted himself up onto his elbow and put both my wrists into his big left hand. With one hand he was able to keep me pinned down securely. He put his other hand between my legs and roughly pushed them apart. He directed the head of his dick to my pussy and gently rubbed just the tip up and down over my soaking wet lips.

"You little fuck," I moaned loudly, and arched up as much

as I could with my arms still pinned back.

"Poor, teasing, princess. Wants a nice hard cock, doesn't she?"

He circled his dick around more.

I wanted to resist him. I wanted to beat his ass more, but my body betrayed me. I'd been staring at that huge cock all evening and I wanted it now.

I nodded up and down in quick agreement.

"*No!*" he said cruelly.

"But it's my birthday?" I pleaded.

He took the dangling leash handle still hanging from his neck and pulled it up in front of me.

"Well here ya go then, Princess. You can feel like you still have some control over what happens."

He pushed the handle of the leash into my still pinned-down hand and then thrust his cock deep into me. I screamed louder than anyone would have ever expected to hear coming from a Disney resort room.

He slowly pulled back out and then thrust down deeply again. I think I might have blacked out for a brief second. He knew exactly what he was doing to me!

I remember hearing a line from an 80's movie asking if a guy could hammer a six-inch spike into the ground with his penis. At that moment, I was pretty sure that Adam possessed the ability to do just that!

But then, he just stopped. I was totally lost in the moment. I looked up at him, and he just smiled. I tried to buck my hips up towards him but he stopped me.

"No. I'm not done with you yet, teasing princess."

He sat up, pulled the leash handle from my hand, and unlocked the leash from his throat. Then he leaned down towards me and slipped the chain back behind my head and quickly clasped it around my neck.

"Come."

He tugged the leash, pulling me up onto my feet. My

nightgown was still pulled up on the bottom and down on the top. It was clinging to me and hardly effective.

He led me into the bathroom. The room had a tiled shower instead of a typical tub and there were several grab bars on the wall lining the inside of the shower. He directed me into the shower stall by the leash, still semi-dressed in the black, silky, fabric. He pressed me face-first to the side wall.

"Lift up your leg."

He tapped on my right leg and I lifted it slightly. As I did, he took hold of my ankle and lifted my leg up so that my foot rested on the bar positioned in a ballerina pose. The water came on. It was cold for a brief second but quickly warmed up. The water ran down over me, causing the black lace to melt against my body. I felt his hand stroking my pussy lips. It was only a brief moment before he was thrusting into me from behind. The warm water sprayed both of our bodies. I pressed my hands against the tile wall as my pussy milked at his cock and pulled it deep inside me.

As I started to feel the wave of orgasms hit me, I heard him growl. It was so animalistic that it made me cum even harder. I could feel him gush into me as his growl became louder.

I lifted my foot from the bar and lowered my leg down. He pressed his chest against my back and my face rested against the tile wall of the shower while we both paused for a few minutes to catch our breath.

I peeled the soaking-wet lace nightgown down off my body and let it fall in a pile onto the shower floor. I stepped out of the shower while Adam stayed and leaned against the wall where my face had just rested.

I pulled down a towel off the rack and briefly became a self-entitled tourist. I didn't even dry off. I unfolded the towel and let it hang vertically in front of me, hugging it to my body with one hand. I dripped a trail of water as I stumbled with trembling legs towards the little kitchenette that was a few steps from the bathroom.

I leaned down, still holding the towel against me with only one hand, and opened the mini-fridge to grab a bottle of water. I quickly cracked the bottle open and put it to my lips.

As my head leaned back, my eyes raised, too. I paused and tried to focus. There, staring at me from across the room on the couch, next to the tray of untouched sex toys, were the fucking smug horse-face pillows looking right at me!

Well-played Disney... well-played.

A Relaxing Vacation
Boardwalk Resort

BLAINE MCKINNON CUSTOM GIN AND TONIC
Belle Vue Lounge, Boardwalk Resort

Crushed Ice
2 oz. Plymouth Gin
4 oz. Fever Tree Tonic Water
1/2 Key Lime, Squeezed
Stirred

FELT LIKE I was starting to forget. I didn't want to forget, but I was. The old EPCOT Center of long ago had all changed. I understood that all the changes were part of "progress" but I wasn't sure if anyone who decided on those changes really knew what progress meant.

I missed loveable Figment from the Journey Into Imagination attraction most. He was as much a part of my childhood as Mickey Mouse. I had a plush Figment that I got on one of our many family trips to Walt Disney World when I was a little girl. I remembered how much I loved that adorable purple dragon, yet, sometimes, I forgot why. It had been so long since I saw him, the real one. I couldn't remember the last time I noticed a child at Epcot who held onto their Figment doll like he was their best friend.

I didn't spend much time in Future World at Epcot anymore. But when I strolled through that part of the park, those were the types of things that I wondered about. I felt nostalgic and depressed. I wanted it back the way it was. I didn't think that there was anyone else in the world who felt that way besides me. As long as there was a Duffy meet 'n' greet with a gift shop, most Guests seemed satisfied.

Somehow, despite the sense of loss over what once was, Epcot still topped the list as my favorite park. I learned to enjoy everything else that it had to offer. I left my childhood memories in Future World and made new adult memories in the World Showcase. I sometimes spent half the day in one country while I explored every hidden detail. I talked to the Cast Members from each country; they always had interesting stories to tell. I also learned a few words in each language from them. I learned to relax there. I learned to slowly browse around in the stores. I learned to try new foods and new drinks. Horizons no longer existed in Future World, but I still expanded my horizons in World Showcase. That is where I went when I needed to escape.

I was having a weekend stay at the Boardwalk Resort to do just that: escape. I spent the afternoon wandering around the World Showcase shops before I grabbed a strawberry tart at the bakery in France and sat at the fountain to people-watch. It was early evening, and I figured that I would head back to the Boardwalk to have a drink at The Belle Vue Lounge after my snack. The adult beverage options throughout the World Showcase were legendary, but there were few places at Walt Disney World that could compare with the calm, quiet, elegance of the Belle Vue.

I wandered back along the path from the International Gateway exit from Epcot to the resort, went upstairs to the lobby level of the Boardwalk, and down the hall to the lounge. As usual, it was pretty quiet there and I liked that. It was nearly empty, which was a shame, but that made it perfect at the same time. There were no restaurants next to it to create excessive traffic overflow or crowds; they were all outside along the boardwalk. It always seemed like the same bartender was there every time I visited. And every time I visited, he still carded me. And every time he carded me his tip got bigger. It just added to the lounge's charm.

On this particular visit, there was only one Guest there. He was kind of cute, for a tourist. He was sitting at a table along the back wall, clutching his drink. He was at the only table in the lounge that had a cocktail menu sitting on it. Of course, I could have just asked the bartender for one, but what kind of adventure would that have been if there was a perfectly good tourist sitting there all alone?

I waved to the bartender as I walked past him to the one occupied table. He gave me a smile and a nod in his typical cordial fashion. I smiled back and went directly to the lone gentleman's table. I stood at the table and looked down at him but he was deep in thought and didn't seem to notice.

"May I borrow your bar menu? I'm looking for something exciting and new."

"Yeah, sure."

He handed the menu up to me and took a sip of his drink. He seemed sad. Maybe he was lonely? I assumed that he was there for a conference. I'd been to the Walt Disney World Resorts often enough that I could usually recognize the difference between Guests who were there for a work versus pleasure trip. He was tense, mentally preoccupied, and alone. Either he was there for business, or he had just run away from home. I didn't know if he was interested in company, but I was. So, I decided to ask.

"Are you expecting someone? I hate to drink alone. I'm going to drink anyway, but I hate to do it alone."

He smiled and motioned towards the seat across from him at the table, and I nodded and sat.

"Thank you. Good company always makes things taste better."

I began to flip through the menu book. "This is a bit frustrating. What happened to all the cool drinks that were themed to the resorts? This is the same generic menu that I see at every resort now. You probably aren't familiar with the days of the monorail cocktails, are you? And don't even get me started on the Kungaloosh."

I sighed in slight frustration and he suddenly perked up. He lifted his head up from his drink and his eyes widened.

"You know about the monorail cocktails?"

"Umm... sure."

"And the Kungaloosh?"

"Of course! I *am* an Adventurer, after all!" I sat up proudly.

"And you're pissed off that they are gone, along with damn near all the originality and theming that used to be what made Walt Disney World, especially EPCOT Center, so awesome?"

"Damn straight!"

He reached out his hand.

"Hi, I'm Blaine."

I extended my hand. "I'm Blu."

"It is a true *pleasure* to meet you, Blu."

"Charmed, I'm sure, Blaine. What are you drinking? Correct me if I'm wrong but I'm guessing it's not off the standard cookie cutter bar menu? It has no glow cube."

He smiled slightly. It was refreshing to see.

"Definitely not! I call it the 'Blaine McKinnon'."

"You named the drink after yourself?"

"Yes, why the fuck not?"

"Good point. So, tell me, what do you taste like?"

"Gin and Tonic!"

"Not exactly what I was expecting, but I'm open to new experiences. I've never had one. I think gin smells like old church-lady perfume."

"This gin and tonic is crushed ice, Plymouth gin, Fever Tree tonic water, and half of a key lime... stirred!"

"Only key limes?"

"*Yes!*"

"That's very detailed."

"I've spent a long time perfecting it."

"Sounds delicious. I'll have two."

We ordered the drinks and talked about the old EPCOT Center and "the good ol' days". It was fantastic to spend an evening chatting with someone who remembered the days of detailed Imagineering, and Cast Members who loved their work and understood the traditions that made Walt Disney

World so magical. Blaine longed for the days before a big wand was stuck on top of Spaceship Earth. But we both agreed that despite the changes, there was still something there. We were attached to it, and we missed it when we weren't there. We mourned the loss of things that changed over the years, but we still constantly needed it. Walt Disney World gave us a fix of something that felt addictive and made us need to be there.

"Are you here for a convention, Blaine? You scream 'business guy', but the fact that you pine over the loss of EPCOT Center throws a wrench in my theory."

"No. Well, I am a business guy. I had my own company. But, I'm taking a break, a very big break. You see, my dog died and he was my best friend. I left my work, and there was this girl who had me all twisted up…."

"I'm sorry to hear that, Blaine, but, at the risk of being rude, you are tip-toeing into country music lyrics territory."

"Okay, I live here. Well, not here. I live over at the Beach Club, across Crescent Lake from here."

"You what? You live *here*? I didn't know that you could do that. You must have had one hell of a company back home Blaine."

"Yes. It was great, but I don't want that right now. I escaped the world and I moved here and I'm not sure when I'm going back. This is the one place where I needed to be. I wanted to come back here and feel what I used to feel. A lot has changed, but I'm still not ready to go back to real life. This was the safest place that I could find to escape."

"Okay, Blaine. I understand. I'm not going to criticize you. We all want to escape sometimes. Most of us just don't have the luxury to do so. I would live here too, if I could. I'm actually a lot more like you than you may realize. I live a few miles from here and I still visit and pay for hotel rooms every couple of weeks just to get my fix and run away from home. So, I'm not going to judge. Just when I think I have my fix of this place, I go home and I barely make it to the next day without looking for reasons to book another trip or go to some special event. I want to go through life feeling like I always do when I'm here. I'm an addict. I don't know how to stay away. But I've also never actually tried."

"Yeah, I've seen a lot of that around here, *a lot*!" Blaine said.

"I've heard there is stuff you can buy to help keep that magical feeling when you go home. I imagine that it's just rumors and wishful thinking. It would be nice to find something to take the edge off so that all my extra cash didn't go towards hotel rooms. I suppose we all have our own personal vice. Right?"

"Yes, I'm sure that's just a fairytale and wishful thinking." Blaine chuckled nervously.

We talked over a second drink and reminisced more. We both agreed that we could probably solve all of Walt Disney World's problems in one night of brainstorming over cocktails. By the third drink, we were ready to take over the World. Blaine was actually laughing. I got the strong impression that he hadn't laughed in a while. The man was stressed!

The drinks were strong and I felt no pain after an hour or two into our discussion. The alcohol combined with the stimulating conversation about EPCOT Center had me feeling frisky. I'm not ashamed to admit that the Disney freak in me has a fetish for guys who know all about it.

"Blaine? Would you like to continue this conversation in my room? It's just down the hall, on the other side of the lobby."

As I leaned in to make my proposal, my top gaped open, slightly revealing my substantial cleavage. He suddenly seemed slightly nervous and stared at my tits without answering.

"Blaine, how about you order two more drinks to go and we'll head out of here so we can put our feet up in my room?"

He nodded and went to the bar to get more drinks. Once they were ready, we left the quiet of the lounge and walked down the hall towards the Boardwalk Resort lobby. We passed by an antique carrousel that sat on top of a round bench seat at the front entrance to the resort. It still spun and played music. I showed Blaine the hidden Mickey on the back leg of one of the horse figurines. He seemed fascinated for a moment, and when it began to play, he sang along with the tunes in a distinctly drunken slurred way.

I pulled him along towards the check-in area of the lobby. It wasn't as large and overwhelming as the lobby in the Grand Floridian Resort or the Wilderness Lodge, but it was still elegant and welcoming. Spending time reading the newspaper on a plush sofa there would be a welcome addition to any relaxing vacation. As we made our way to the end of the lobby near the gift shop, we both pointed to the creepy chairs on the sides of the fireplace at the same time. We paused for a moment with tilted heads and stared at them.

"What were they thinking? Those always creep me out," Blaine said.

"It's art. I did a tour here not long ago; they're called nanny chairs. During the turn of the century, the adults sat on them while the kids rode the carrousel in old amusement parks."

"They have faces."

"They were on kids' rides. I guess they're supposed to be whimsical."

"Dear God."

"I wonder how many children contemplated becoming serial killers after a childhood full of staring at those things? That can't be healthy. Maybe we should keep moving along?"

"Fuckin' creepy," Blaine mumbled.

"You have a very dirty mouth, Blaine."

"Yes. I'm kind of proud of it."

"You should be. I like that in a man. Especially here in the land of pixie dust. It adds some balance."

We arrived at my room and went inside. I had a one-bedroom villa with a gorgeous view of the boardwalk and lake. It was the third time they had given me the same room upon check-in. I wished that I could just move into it permanently like Blaine had at the Beach Club. It was the perfect location. I was on the main lobby level and just above the Screen Door shop on the corner.

"Please, make yourself at home, Blaine."

It didn't take long for him to do just that. He sat on the couch, kicked off his shoes, and reclined his body back while stretching his arms out wide. He took a sip of his drink and spilled a few drops onto his shirt. I had no idea how many drinks he'd had before I joined him at the lounge, but it was obvious that he had definitely found his happy place.

I walked away from the couch and looked through the window. It was nearly impossible to see much from inside, so I opened the door to the balcony. The music drifted up from inside the store below. It was different from what was being played on the boardwalk. Having my room directly above the store made this a special place for exclusive turn-of-the-century tunes. It was just another reason why I adored it there.

I stepped out onto the balcony. There were only a few people outside. It must have been about seven o'clock because the nighttime entertainment of live street performer shows had started. Just below my balcony, a man was setting up props for a show. He was very thin and wore a pair of funny checkered pants with suspenders. A half-dozen Guests stood around watching him unload props from a massive suitcase.

I walked back into the room and noticed that Blaine's mood had definitely changed for the better since I'd stumbled across him in the lounge. He was sprawled out on the couch with his head back and his arms stretched out as his foot tapped along with the music. Earlier in the evening, I'd cut him off when he began to ramble about his dog and a girl, so I wasn't sure of the details of what had him all messed up. It was good to see him so relaxed. I had never met someone who was in such desperate need to unwind as my new EPCOT Center-loving friend.

I walked over to him and put a knee on either side of his

legs, straddling his lap and pinning him back onto the couch. He lifted his head up, smiled at me, then took another sip of his drink. I took the glass out of his hand while it was still raised up to his mouth.

"Here, let me help you with that."

I drank the remainder of his gin and tonic, then leaned in to kiss him. As our lips met, I dropped the glass onto the floor next to the couch and ran both my hands up through his hair. We broke from the kiss. I could feel a hardness pressing up between my thighs. I adjusted myself on his lap to take advantage of it.

"Are you trying to take advantage of my being drunk? Are you trying to seduce me?"

"You're very cute, Blaine, but you need to relax or you're going to snap."

"*Fuckin'* right I do! That *is* why I came here!"

"Yes, exactly, but it's not enough to just sit at a pool all day, Blaine. That's not going to relax you the way that you really need."

"Snow White left me! Fuck! Why won't she just come back?"

"Shhhhh, Blaine. It's okay. You'll find your Snow White one day. Tonight, you can relax with me."

I held his face in my hands. He mumbled a drunken slur that I couldn't make out, then pulled me close to him for a kiss. The strong scent of gin lingered between us. I bit lightly at his lip and he ran his hands up onto my tits while slipping his tongue deeper into my mouth. We stayed locked in the kiss as we heatedly pulled at each other's clothing until I heard threads tear. I pulled back a few inches. My lips still hovered closely to his.

"You need to be fucked, Blaine."

He let out a sigh and seemed to involuntarily press his hips up against me, between my legs.

"Yessss, yes I *do*!" he groaned.

I leaned closer to his ear. "Do you want me to fuck you, Blaine?"

He moaned softly and his kisses became more aggressive. I lifted up my dress then scrambled to unzip his jeans. Suddenly, there were sounds of clapping behind me and I looked over my shoulder, bewildered. Blaine laid back against the couch and raised his arms up clapping above his head

"Yayyyyy! Applause! Applause!" he said.

The gin was definitely enhancing his mood.

"It's the show down on the boardwalk. Nothing like fucking to a round of applause, huh, Blaine?"

"That *does* sound encouraging... and... supportive," he slurred at me.

"Well, I'm all for being encouraging and supportive."

I slid off of Blaine's lap and pulled him up to follow me to the balcony. The balcony enclosure was built as a solid structure wall with no slats or rails; it was also higher than most. It came up to my chest. It gave complete privacy, at least from the waist down. We both looked out over the balcony at the performer entertaining a handful of Guests below. He noticed us, looked up, and waived. We waived back.

"Maybe he could use someone entertaining him for a change?" I said.

I turned around to face Blaine and gave him another kiss. I leaned with my back against the balcony wall and he put his hands on my hips, running them up and down over me as he kissed me more.

"Fuck me right here on the balcony in front of him, Blaine."

He was quick to agree. He kissed down my neck and sunk his teeth into me. I felt the wetness between my legs build. I reached down to complete the mission that I had begun on the couch. I wanted to feel the hard bulge that was teasing me.

"Please fuck me in front of him, Blaine. Let yourself go. Just relax and have fun. You need this."

That was all the encouragement that he needed. He spun

me around and pushed my face and shoulders down so that I was leaning onto the ledge of the balcony wall. I felt him put a hand on either side of my thighs and raise my dress up over my hips. A light breeze teased across my bare ass as he exposed me. He slid his hands from my hips up over my ass and dug them into the milky flesh.

I looked down towards the boardwalk below us and at the performer. He was interacting with Guests and preparing to juggle bowling pins. The Guests surrounding him had their backs to us, but the performer was in our direct line of vision. It was unavoidable. He was our entertainment and we were his.

Blaine teased his dick up and down my wet pussy while I remained bent over in front of him. I looked back at him over my shoulder, and I could tell that he was savoring the moment. Like a man who was starving and just stumbled upon a buffet, he didn't seem to know where to start.

"Fuck. Me. Blaine."

He pressed his hardness into me in one firm stroke. I gasped and let out a low moan. His fingers dug into my hips as he paused. I was sure he was just taking a moment to enjoy the comfort of a cozy, wet, pussy, but it teased me too much for him to fill me like that and then just stand there motionless. I slowly started to move back on him. I circled and grinded my hips then gently started sliding. He followed my lead and pumped into me in short little strokes, then fully to the hilt. He teased me with just the tip, then fucked me in deep strokes again. It was a horrible shame that he had been going through a dry spell. He was a serious fucking-champ!

I opened my eyes and looked down at the street performer while Blaine started pumping into me more. My tits bounced but were hidden by the solid balcony. The slapping sounds of us fucking were luckily drowned out by the Screen Door shop music. I bit onto my lip and held onto the ledge tighter. I was thoroughly enjoying the benefit of Blaine's new relaxation efforts.

I glanced up again and tried to make eye contact with the performer. I noticed he had pulled out a bowling ball and pins. He spent some time balancing two chairs on top of one another. Once the chairs were secure, he climbed on top of the stack and began tossing two pins back and forth. I pressed back onto Blaine's dick harder. My pussy clenched around him and milked his dick with each stroke.

"Hot-fucking-damn, I needed this," he blurted out.

I smiled and rocked back and forth faster, attempting to not lose myself completely. I stared down at the performer, trying to will him to look back at me. I wanted him to notice us fucking despite the balcony. He continued to toss the pins back and forth and then added the bowling ball into the mix.

I felt a forceful shove from Blaine as he let out a loud moan. I quickly pressed my face into my arm to muffle the sound but before I could stop, the performer looked up. The performer's eyes suddenly widened and it was clear that he lost focus as he realized what he was seeing. His hands scrambled, trying to keep up his juggling rhythm before he dropped everything!

Bowling pins bounced and flew into the air while Guests chased after them in an attempt to help. The bowling ball bounced twice, then cracked and shattered into a bunch of small pieces. I let out a shocked laugh that immediately turned to moans as Blaine began to fuck me even harder.

While chaos reigned below us, we both started to moan and cum.

Blaine collapsed forward onto my back and rested his head near my shoulder. I could hear him panting. I felt the warm air on my back. The scent of gin still drifted up from his rapid breath.

The handful of Guests who watched the live boardwalk show wandered away at the end of the glorious finale disaster. The performer stood alone, surrounded by broken bowling ball pieces. He slouched his head and sulked.

Blaine lifted his head from my back and looked down at him from over my shoulder.

"That guy really needs to relax."

Red-Headed Geisha
Japan, Epcot

ORANGE SAKE COCKTAIL
Outdoor Sake Bar, Japan, Epcot

Minute Maid Orange Smoothie Mix
Sake to Taste

I HAD NOT SEEN Michael in nearly two years, since meeting him at a D23 Expo in California. During the event, he approached me while I waited in a hopeless line to see Dick Van Dyke. He commented that I was "too cute to look so sad," then pulled me out of the line and took me straight in to have a seat with him. I quickly learned that Michael did *not* wait in lines; he lived life a bit differently than anyone else I knew. He was the owner and CEO of a major pharmaceutical company. He had more money than most people could imagine. His every step was VIP: he ate the best food, stayed in the presidential suites, had on-call staff wherever he went, and even had a full-time driver who doubled as his security guard. He worked hard, and played harder.

Every few months, he would call me to catch up while he was alone and bored in a hotel room on business. He never had time for a wife or serious relationship. Work always came first, but he did enjoy having companionship. The fact that we were both Disney fanatics created a special bond. He knew that he could always call me, flirt, talk Disney, and wind down after a rough day.

Although I've always been a rather independent woman, Michael enjoyed spoiling me. Since we'd met in California, he'd always sent me elaborate gifts for holidays and my birthday. It made him happy to pamper me. And after the first time that he sent an expensive piece of jewelry (that I refused to sign for), I realized it was a waste of energy to resist. He had it hand-delivered every day for two months before I finally accepted. He was a determined man. He never accepted "no" for an answer.

So when I got a call from him saying that he would be at Walt Disney World, not only was I excited to see him in person again, but I knew it would be an over-the-top adventure. I met him at the Animal Kingdom Lodge the afternoon that he arrived. Of course he was staying in the Royal Asante Presidential Suite. I was so excited to see him again, but when he opened the door of the suite, I barely returned his hug before being overwhelmed by the room.

"*Wow!*" was all I could say as I walked into the suite with my jaw dropped.

"I take it you approve? Look around. There's a lot to take in. Disney outdid themselves with this room, I have to admit," Michael said.

There was a huge dining table off the front foyer that looked like it was made out of a cross-cut section of a massive tree. The living room was round with a high ceiling, a view of the animals on the savannah, and a remote-controlled fireplace. I started running around the suite finding amazing things at each turn. Then I stumbled upon the master bedroom. At the far end of the room was a poster bed covered in cream-colored gauze netting. The frame looked like it was made from several tree trunks. It was elegant and rustic at the same time. It was amazing. I walked towards it, but before I reached it, I felt my arm tugged back to spin me around.

"Long time no see, my dear."

Before I could respond, Michael pulled me to him and placed his soft lips to mine. I was instantly lost in his passionate kisses. He led me back a few steps towards the bed. I leaned against the corner bedpost and passionately kissed him back, running my hands up over his chest and down again. I thought he was going to take me right there on that piece of artwork pretending to be a bed, but he released me from the kiss. I wrapped my arms around his neck. My leg ran up and down the outside of his. I wanted him now.

"You tempt me so much, dear girl. There will be plenty of time for that later."

"You tempt me even more, dear man, but as you wish."

He led me back to the living room and we sat down to talk over a glass of wine. After we caught up, we decided to head to Epcot for dinner. I knew it wasn't the best food on property, but my favorite view of *Illuminations* was from a window table inside Tokyo Dining in Japan. I loved the full wall of glass windows overlooking the water as I sat elevated above all of the crowd. I had recently discovered that spot and was really surprised by how beautiful it was. I told Michael that despite his preference for a more high-end dining experience, I'd love to share the view with him.

He indulged me by calling the concierge to make a reservation. A few minutes later, everything Michael wanted was confirmed and we left the decadent suite to spend the evening in Epcot.

A car waited for us at the entrance of the resort. I was impressed, but not even slightly surprised. The thought of Michael waiting for a bus made me giggle as we got into the car. We drove to Epcot but never went to the main gate. The driver took us in through a back entrance with a security booth instead of a toll plaza. As we entered the area, I heard racing sounds.

I glanced up. A car raced by inside a small road that circled above us. I could see up through the center of the open-circle track. It looked like a bigger version of a Hot Wheels racetrack.

"Hey! That's Test Track! I've never been backstage at Epcot."

"Personally, I prefer the direct route to the attractions," Michael responded.

"Yes. We both know that you do not like to wait."

The car moved slowly along the narrow road that circles behind the World Showcase. I looked around, trying to take everything in. Unfortunately, it was a sea of big steel buildings and machinery. It was nothing fancy at all. I didn't expect backstage to be so industrial. I was still fascinated, but I definitely preferred the side of the park with the special "Disney magic". The novelty of steel buildings and dumpsters quickly wore off.

We pulled into the back of the Japan Pavilion near the Mitsukoshi shop. Although the view wasn't as magical as entering through the front entrance of the park and seeing Spaceship Earth, the backstage route was a lot more convenient.

We had a couple of hours before dinner, so we decided to enjoy the store and the architecture of the pavilion. The unfortunate part of our special date was that I couldn't relax when I went out with Michael. Well, I could relax with Michael if we were alone in his room, but out in the open public his security guard always followed. Michael never seemed to care; I supposed he was used to it. It was difficult for me to relax with someone always watching, though.

In a way, part of me felt sorry for Michael. He was a charming, handsome man with all the money in the world, but he had no real freedom. It was the price he chose to pay.

We browsed through the back of the store that showcased several shelves of Japanese snacks. There were exotic things that most likely sat there for ages. I didn't see anyone racing to purchase candied baby crabs or fish. I held up some of the various treats, smiled, and waved my hand in front of them in model-fashion as I presented each one to Michael.

"Michael, would you care for some super-yummy dried squid?"

"No, thank you. I think I'll pass this time. I don't want to spoil my appetite for dinner."

"Ooooh, the candied baby crabs look delicious! How about these?"

"How about I buy them for you and we go sit outside until I watch you eat the entire bag?"

"Well, as tempting as that sounds, I don't want to spoil my dinner either. Maybe next time."

I carefully put the bag back on the shelf. Michael enjoyed having control, and he even saw playful banter as a challenge. If I taunted him more, I had no doubt that the rest of the evening would involve me pouting with a mouth full of baby crabs. I left the snack area and wandered through the next few sections of the store.

"Michael, look how beautiful these are. So feminine. I *love* them."

We entered into a room lined with beautiful kimonos. There were all types of colors and designs. They hung on bars mounted around the perimeter of the room. A small section of gowns was roped off. The gracious Japanese Cast Members who worked in that section of the store explained that those particular kimonos were made from expensive fine silk. I admired the designs and the shimmer of the fabric.

"They look so soft," I whispered to myself.

Michael was off to the side of the room having a conversation with the shop girls. I was too distracted looking through the beautiful silk garments to listen to what they talked about. A moment later the girls approached me, bowed, and gestured towards the silk kimonos.

"Welcome to Japan. You like to try?"

"They are very lovely."

"Thank you very much." She bowed again. "You choose one."

"No, no thank you. I'm just looking."

Michael interrupted. "Choose one."

"What?"

"Choose one."

Michael stood tall with his arms crossed over in front of him. The expression on his face was one of determination. It was obvious that the topic was not up for discussion.

I turned towards the section of silk kimonos and pulled out the one that had immediately caught my attention. It was made of an off-white colored silk, with pink cherry blossom designs that were offset by some wisps of brown cherry blossom stems. It was more than pretty. It was luscious, luxurious, and downright gorgeous.

The two shop girls led me towards the center of the room in front of Michael (as well as the other Guests). I stood in place as they dressed me. I was wearing a short sundress, but they simply slipped the kimono over it. I chose a pink sash from a display in the center of the room. As they wrapped it around me, I spun around in front of Michael giggling like a little girl playing dress-up. Within a few minutes, they had me covered in head-to-toe soft silk.

One of the Japanese girls walked off and quickly returned with some odd-looking socks and a pair of very uncomfortable-looking wooden shoes. She pulled over a chair from the corner of the room and invited me to sit. She gingerly removed my sandals and put the socks and shoes on me. The socks had a divider in them so that my big toe was separated from the rest of my toes. The wooden shoes had a strap like flip flops that could be worn with the socks.

While I sat there, the other girl pulled all my hair up and twirled it into a bun. She pulled decorative hair pins from a display and worked them into the bun to hold it in place. My favorite was a long stick that had glass beads and a pink butterfly dangling from the end. The butterfly appeared to be in mid-flight, fluttering around my head.

As they finished dressing me, I retrieved my compact and lipstick from my purse. I powdered my already-pale skin and freshened up my red lips to get in to the spirit. I glanced up at Michael. His arms were still crossed, but now he was smiling proudly.

"My beautiful, red-headed, geisha doll."

I smiled, giggled, and covered my mouth pretending to be shy for his amusement. He chuckled, but it was obvious that he was not convinced of my innocence.

We both thanked the lovely girls who assisted us, and in return they bowed repeatedly and thanked us as well.

Michael then took me by the arm and led me into the next section of the store. For a moment, as I wandered past all the casually dressed tourists, I felt all eyes on me as if I was on display. Michael must have sensed that I had suddenly become uneasy.

"You look beautiful."

"Thank you, Michael."

"This is the most relaxed I've felt in quite some time. I hope you are having fun. This *is* supposed to be fun. Are you having fun, my dear?"

I paused for a moment before I responded. Michael was right. I was dressed in beautiful clothes, pampered by a gorgeous man, and spending time in my most favorite place in the entire world. I began to smile ear to ear.

"Yes Michael, I'm having a blast!"

There was a lot of loud banging and yelling at the far end of the shop. We walked towards the distant sounds. I held firmly onto Michael's arm while attempting to walk in the awkward wooden shoes. I knew that the noise came from the counter where Guests pick an oyster for a pearl to make into jewelry. I assumed he was going to let me pick one. But we only stood there for a brief moment before he turned me back around to walk in the direction that we had come.

We were halfway back to the kimono room when he suddenly turned and pulled me into a small room hidden off to the right side of the shop. I nearly fell, but he held me steady as I regained my balance. I looked around. I knew the room, but had only stopped in out of curiosity once or twice before.

"Oh no, Michael. Don't even think about it."

He pulled me close to him and looked down at me.

"Do you really want to deny me this pleasure?"

I looked away but he put his hand to my chin and lifted my face back up. His eyes stared right through me.

"Let me have this," he said in a soft, but powerful tone.

We were standing in a small nook of a store lined with some of the finest pearl jewelry that I had ever seen. Each item was displayed under glass. The room had a soft warm glow from the backlighting. A purchase from this room was an unheard of indulgence for the typical Disney tourist. Michael looked around and made his mind up quickly.

He presented me with a stunning pearl bracelet and placed it onto my wrist. It was beautiful. Michael was smiling. I was speechless.

Again, he took my arm and we walked past the yelling, banging, pick-a-pearl display. To the left were big walls of Hello Kitty dolls, clothing, and accessories. I picked up one of the small scented erasers from an end-cap display of novelty school supplies and showed it to Michael.

"You know, my parents bought me Hello Kitty stuff at Disney before it was trendy. I don't remember ever seeing Hello Kitty things anywhere else. No other kids had them at school. I was young enough that I remember looking at the display table and it was at my eye level. I had to reach up to touch anything on the table. My parents would buy me one of these scented erasers, or mini pencils, or fancy paper each trip. It was all just stationary store stuff. No stuffed animals or clothing that I can recall. I'm sure I would have remembered huge stuffed plush dolls like they have here. I think we bought the souvenirs at Downtown Disney, but it was still Disney Shopping Village then. Epcot didn't even exist yet."

I put the eraser down and Michael led me towards the exit of the store.

"Michael, wait. I'm in all these clothes! What about the bracelet?"

"It's fine. I've got a tab with the store."

"Of course you do," I said, nodding.

I still had not adapted to how different a visit to Disney World was with Michael. We walked out the door and towards the small standalone sake bar that sat outside. Michael looked at the menu.

"Would you like a drink before dinner? We should fully embrace the spirit of Japan and enjoy something. Perhaps a frozen beer or sake?"

"No frozen beer. Yuck."

"How about a sake cocktail?"

"That sounds delicious. There's an orange sake cocktail. It's perfect for your vacation. It's Japanese *and* Florida all at once!"

"I love your logic."

Michael laughed at me and turned to the girl behind the counter at the bar to place our order. We took our drinks with us as we strolled through the pavilion. I was finally learning to balance as I walked on the wooden Japanese shoes, but Michael seemed to enjoy having a red-headed geisha close by so I stayed on his arm anyway.

We watched Guests feed crackers to the fish in the pond and then walked up the incline that led to the quick-service restaurant. We paused for quite some time to admire the bonsai trees.

"They are so beautiful and delicate. And before you even start to think about it Michael, no! I do not want one!"

"Okay! Okay! No bonsai tree. But why not? It's almost as beautiful as you."

"Because I will kill it."

"What? Why?"

"Oh, I don't want to kill it, but I will kill it. Every plant I've owned died a horrible, slow, death. So, please, do not place that suffering on such a beautiful thing."

"Okay. If you put it that way, I understand."

Michael leaned down and kissed me on my powdered forehead. I betrayed the spirit of the shy geisha by wrapping my arms around his neck and pulling him down further. I placed a small kiss on the tip of his nose before realizing how much lipstick I was wearing. I rubbed my finger on his nose in an attempt to remove it.

"Oops. I'm sorry. You look like Rudolph!"

"You know how much I love your whore-red lipstick. Not necessarily on my nose, but it's easy to forgive you when your lips look so tempting."

I fluttered my eyes at him, covered my mouth, and giggled.

"That innocent giggle still isn't working, but I enjoy watching you try to pull it off. I just know that if I had you alone, you'd go quickly from shy, giggling girl to pleasure slave without batting your pretty lashes. In fact...."

Michael took me by the arm and pulled me behind him to follow. I stumbled a bit in the shoes, but recovered quickly and walked as best as I could with him pulling me along.

"Michael, what are you doing?"

He glanced over his shoulder at me as we hurried along. "I'm enjoying the company of a geisha."

He had a gleam in his eye that concerned, yet excited me. We headed back down the main path towards the far entrance of the store.

"Does that mean we're leaving?"

"No!"

We walked over the bridge leading to the shop but never went inside. He turned left into the small museum room located in the foyer of the store. I was hit with a blast of frigid air-conditioning as we entered the room. There were two people in there looking at the glass-encased exhibits. Michael directed me to one of the long bench seats surrounding a Zen garden in the middle of the room.

"Sit."

I did as he instructed, quietly and without question. He promptly left the room and I waited.

The two people in the room left a few moments later. I'd been in this mini museum many times before. It had interesting things, like origami birds and anime items. Today I chose to stay seated instead of looking for new exhibits.

Michael returned a few minutes later holding a small bag. He walked towards me, determined. He stopped in front of me, hovering. He didn't have to say anything. I reached out to him and opened his pants.

I licked my lips with anticipation as I leaned in towards his hard dick. I placed light kisses on the tip, then onto his balls. I pressed my tongue to the base of his cock, looked directly up at him, and slowly trailed my tongue up his entire length.

"Mmmmm, my little geisha doll," he moaned.

I kissed the tip of his cock gently, then plunged my mouth down over it, completely taking him in. My red lips slid up and down until he pulled back from me. I enjoyed hearing him gasp for breath.

"Spread your legs," he said.

I lifted the kimono along with my dress underneath and sat with the cold, hard, wood of the seat against my bare skin. I opened my legs wide and ran my hand down towards my pussy.

"I knew that you would be a perfect geisha. You know how to provide pleasure, my dear."

I stroked my pussy in front of him and teased myself with my fingers. He reached for the bag that was sitting next to me on the bench and pulled out a set of fancy chopsticks decorated with cherry blossom flowers that matched my kimono.

"Open your mouth, pretty girl."

I looked up at him and opened my mouth slightly. He teased across my lips with the thick end of the chopsticks.

"Suck."

I closed my red lips around them and licked. I wanted his

hard cock back in my mouth instead. I closed my eyes and thought of it while I fingered my pussy, and licked around the chopsticks imagining that they were his cock.

Michael slowly pulled the chopsticks from my mouth and lowered himself down onto the floor. I leaned back to allow him better access as I pulled up the kimono fabric more. He placed the broad tip of the wet chopsticks at the entrance of my pussy and teased them up and down.

I moaned softly as he toyed with me. I wanted more.

"Please?"

Michael always appreciated when I begged. The chopsticks slowly entered me and he began to rub them inside.

"You're my dinner appetizer."

His face pressed between my legs and he hungrily licked and bit at my clit. He continued to chopstick-fuck me as I moaned and begged for more.

"Please, please take me. I've wanted you all day! Please! I need you to fuck me, please?"

He sat back on his knees and pet my wet pussy while he continued to tease me. I felt the chopsticks slowly pull out of me. He nearly forced me to cum when he twirled them around as he removed them.

His hand rested on my pussy as I moaned.

"Not yet, my dear girl."

He lifted the soaked chopsticks to his mouth. I didn't think I could want him more until I watched as he sucked them both clean. He was so fucking sexy.

He stood up while taking my hand and pulling me to my feet. I held my skirt up with my free hand. I knew what was going to happen and I wanted it. I needed it.

He shoved the chopsticks into the decorated bun of hair piled on top of my head then dragged me over to the wall. My back went against it as he pinned me with his hard chest. I ran my hands up and down his body, along his neck, and through his hair. He pulled up my left leg. The tease was soon over as he entered me.

He held me in place and mounted me down onto his cock. I balanced on one foot in the hard, wooden shoes, bouncing up and down on his delicious dick. As he got closer to cumming, he started thrusting harder, bucking my whole body into the wall. My hair fell loose from the clips as he groaned with pleasure.

As soon as I felt his hot liquid shoot into me, I moaned out. My muscles clenched around him and pulsed hard. I loved being his pleasure doll.

He held me tightly pressed against the wall for a minute. We were both panting and sweating despite the chill in the room. He released me and helped slide the kimono back down to cover me. I was still shaking as I tried to straighten myself up. I sat back down on the bench and pulled out my compact and lipstick again. Before I even looked in the mirror, I could tell that I was a freshly-fucked mess. Michael reached over to me and stroked the back of his hand down my face.

"Not such a pretty geisha now, am I?"

"You're lovely, my dear. It's about time for dinner."

I quickly powdered my face and reapplied the whore-red lipstick that I knew he loved. I pinned up my hair as best I could and reinserted all the different clips, including the new cherry blossom chopsticks.

Michael reached out his hand to me.

"Shall we go?"

"Yes, but one more thing first."

I pulled him closer to me while I remained seated. I undid his pants again then slid them down to rest around his knees. He didn't question me. He just smiled down at me, watching.

I leaned in just below his delicious cock that had just fucked me so well and nuzzled my nose to his inner thigh. I pressed my lips to his thigh and kissed. I raised my head back up and admired my work. A full, red, lipstick print adorned his upper thigh.

"There. Now I'm ready."

- Michael laughed as he pulled up his pants.

"You are a lovely geisha, my dear."

We walked towards the exit of the museum. Suddenly, a lot of questions were answered. Michael's guard was standing at the doorway to ensure our privacy. He was also holding a huge Hello Kitty plush that he handed to me as I passed by.

I thanked him, smiled, and tried not to laugh. I should not have been surprised. I was still not accustomed to the lifestyle that Michael led.

"Thank you, Michael. You spoil me."

"It is truly my pleasure."

We walked outside towards the restaurant and, as we did, I could feel the warm cum slowly trailing down my inner thigh. I lowered my face into the huge doll and covered my mouth as I felt a blush come over my cheeks.

Michael looked at me. For the first time since we'd met, he was genuinely surprised by my reaction.

"You're blushing! This time I actually believe it."

We took the elevator up to the restaurant. Michael didn't want me to break my neck navigating the steep staircase with the wooden flip flops. As the elevator doors opened on the top floor, I saw a line of Japanese girls all wearing kimonos and bowing.

"Welcome to Japan. Welcome to Japan," they all said repeatedly.

"Michael, where is everyone? Are they closing?"

The restaurant was empty of any other Guests.

"I wanted to make sure that we had a window seat for *Illuminations*. So, I bought out the restaurant for the night."

"Of course you did."

The Caveman Challenge
Ellen's Energy Adventure

COFFEE WITH KAHLUA
Coffee Cart Near Ellen's Energy Adventure, Epcot

Strong Coffee (hot or iced)
Shot of Kahlua Coffee Liquor

I WALKED OUT OF the restroom behind Innoventions and towards Ellen's Energy Adventure. I kept my hand in the side pocket of my dress and rubbed my thumb back and forth across the soft fabric that I held balled up in my hand. I passed by the wait times sign in front of Mission: Space and noticed that Imagination had a five minute wait time.

"That sign would never say five minutes if we had our old, loveable Figment and Dreamfinder back," I murmured to myself.

I'll never understand why someone decided to change that attraction. I'll also never understand why someone else *approved* it! Out of frustration, I squeezed the fabric in my pocket again and redirected my thoughts to happier fantasies. All it took was this "one little spark" to make my imagination run wild with what was about to happen. I became very excited.

I could see Jake sitting on the edge of the planter that surrounded the Ellen's Energy Adventure attraction entrance sign. He was playing on his cell phone and waiting for me to return. He didn't even realize that I was back until I was standing directly in front of him.

"Close your eyes," I said to him.

"Why are you smiling so much? Should I be worried? I'm worried."

"Just close your eyes, Jake. I promise it will be okay. I cross my heart."

Jake tilted his head sideways and slipped his phone into his pocket. He sat up straight and closed his eyes.

"Now, keep your eyes closed."

I pulled my hand out of my pocket. The balled up fabric peeked out from between my fingers. I touched it to Jake's mouth and nose. He jolted back at first, surprised by the touch, and then sat perfectly still. His cheeks rose slightly. I could tell that he was smiling.

"You are such a slut," Jake mumbled through the fabric while keeping his eyes tightly closed.

"You can open your eyes now."

He opened his eyes slowly. I pulled my hand away from his face then opened it in front of him so that he was able to catch a glimpse of the soft pink fabric with little white polka dots.

"When I was in the bathroom, I decided that I didn't need to wear my panties anymore. Do you think I need to wear panties today, Jake?"

Jake didn't respond. He just shook his head "*no*" vigorously. He pulled me closer to him so that I was standing between his legs while he sat. I put the panties back into my dress pocket and placed my arms around the back of Jake's neck.

"I hear the 'No Panties in the Parks' trend is really taking off all over Walt Disney World."

"Is that so?" Jake chuckled.

I nodded. "Yep!"

"Is it your goal to always have me rock hard when we are in the parks?"

"You figured me out! That *is* my goal. In fact, your rock-hard cock has become my favorite attraction in all of the parks!"

"Maybe I should set it up as a meet 'n' greet?"

"I want a Fastpass for that!"

Jake laughed and I could feel his cock press against my thigh. I was ready to drag him into a companion restroom and have my way with him, but I resisted. Jake was always a good sport about being creative on our adventures. He was on his second round with the Disney College Program and very open-minded when it came to fulfilling my fantasies. I found out over the years that the young College Program Cast Members were the most adventurous playmates. I took advantage of that fact as often as possible with him.

"So, since we're here, do you want to go into Ellen's Energy Adventure?"

"I thought you wanted me to stay hard all the time?"

"Come on, Jake! It has dinosaurs! You can pretend that you're a caveman and pull my hair."

"That *is* always fun." Jake reached up and twirled a bit of my long red hair around in his fingertips. "But, Energy is my spot to take a nice air-conditioned nap."

"Well, we could always go over to Journey Into Imagination. The time sign said it only has a five minute wait. Do you wanna do that instead?" I said in an overly-enthusiastic tone.

Jake smirked, "Fine, we'll do Energy. At least Bill Nye, Science Guy, is cool. Oh, and Jamie Lee Curtis is smokin'!"

"Don't forget about Alex Trebec. He still has his old porn mustache in there."

"Why do you have to keep killing it for me?"

"Sorry, Jake. How about I make it up to you?"

"Does that mean we're going into the companion bathroom to fuck now, instead?"

"No."

"Then what?"

"How about we play a game? Are you up for a challenge?"

"You're scaring me again, but it's making my dick twitch. So, yes! Yes! I want a challenge. Please tell me this challenge ends with me fucking you in the companion restroom."

"You really have a one-track mind, Jake."

He looked down at his crotch and motioned to the bulge in his pants.

"Point taken," I said.

"Too bad it's gonna go away if we go into Energy. Ellen is great, but not exactly help for keeping the blood flow going. My dick will be soft in no time." Jake looked at me with pleading puppy dog eyes.

"Are you so sure it will?" I responded slyly.

"Sounds like this is part of the challenge."

"Yes! Here is the challenge: we will ride Energy, and while we are on the ride, no matter what I do, you have to stay soft. If you can get through the entire ride from the time that we sit down in the ride vehicle until the lights come on at the end, you win."

"I win? A soft dick doesn't sound like a win to me. What's the prize?"

"You get to fuck me... any hole."

"I *accept*!"

"Wait. Wait. Don't you want to know what I get if you lose?"

"I'm not going to lose."

"You really think that you can be next to me in the dark for thirty minutes and I won't be able to make your dick stand at attention? It hasn't relaxed the entire time that we've been talking here."

Jake looked down at his crotch again. "Okay, what happens if I lose?"

"I'm gonna ride your face like you are Duffy Bear and I'm trying to rip your head off."

"Ouch! Vicious!"

"Well, you did say that you were setting up a dick meet 'n' greet. I'm just hoping for extra pixie dust during my Guest experience."

"But Duffy Bear?"

"Do you realize how much I want to suffocate that soulless, fluffy fuck?"

"Why is this turning me on?"

"Because even hate-fucks can be fun?"

"That must be it!"

I took Jake by the hand.

He protested. "Wait, I'm not ready yet! I need to calm down!"

"Don't worry. You'll have the preshow time to calm down."

"Oh yeah, Alex Trebec's porn mustache for two hundred, please."

We headed into the attraction. It was utterly empty.

"Typical," said Jake. "Dinosaurs are cool, but they only get you so far. This place really needs an update."

"Yeah, a friend of mine said that the last time he was in here, he could have been naked and standing up on the ride singing *The Star-Spangled Banner* and nobody would have heard or cared."

The preshow was already at the part where Ellen wakes up from her dream when we entered. It was nearly over, and it was about time to move into the ride loading area.

"Sorry that you don't have much time to relax, Jake."

"I'm okay. This place is depressing." Jake shrugged.

The preshow concluded and we followed the Cast Member's instructions to move into the ride loading area and take a seat. There were two huge ride vehicles that could each hold about one hundred people. It was empty. We were it. It was like taking a flight and having the entire plane to yourself. We chose the car on the right side and sat three rows from the back. It was almost eerie looking out over all those rows of seats with not a single person sitting in them.

As we got settled in, Jake began negotiating the terms of our challenge.

"You can't touch me," Jake said confidently.

"Okay," I laughed. "Any other demands?"

"You gotta give me a chance," he pleaded.

I smiled. The room went dark.

I whispered, "I'll need to make sure that you aren't cheating, Jake. Unzip, please."

I heard Jake unzip his jeans slowly.

"I love that sound. It makes me want to grab hold of that delicious hunk of meat and shove it down my throat."

"Son of a bit-," Ellen and Bill Nye popped up on a movie screen in front of us and Jake paused. "Thank *God*!"

Ellen and Bill were holding flashlights similar to those used to guide planes on a runway.

"Jake, do you think those would make good dildos?"

"You do *not* play fair. Luckily the freezing cold air-conditioning draft blowing across my bare balls right now is working in my favor! I never thought I'd be happy about shrinkage."

"You know, two of those lights would be great for some fun glow-in-the-dark double penetration," I said bluntly.

Jake leaned forward with his head in his hands and then took a deep breath and sat back up.

I giggled.

Jake watched the movie introduction with Bill and Ellen talking about fossil fuels. I enjoyed watching Jake more than the movie. He had such a determined look of concentration on his face. It was very amusing, and arousing.

"You can relax, Jake. You don't have to memorize everything they say. There won't be a quiz."

Jake took another deep breath and slowly released it. He glanced at me for a brief moment, then sat up straight, looking forward. Our ride-car started to move into the first room of the attraction. It was filled with audio-animatronic dinosaurs. I always got a kick out of this scene. It reminded me of the old *Land of the Lost* show from when I was a kid, right down to the misty fog filling the air. It was so mysterious.

"Jake, you would look so good in a caveman loincloth. With your muscle-covered, young, tight, body...."

"Stop it!" he hissed.

"I'm imagining it now. You grabbing me by the hair, dragging me into the jungle, tearing my clothes off, and fucking me like a wild animal. You'd just be grunting with this primitive lust and wouldn't even speak. It would be so fucking hot. We should do that sometime."

Jake turned his head towards me. The vein in his forehead was showing.

"I'm ignoring you," Jake snapped. "I'm thinking of stepping on Legos and Bambi's mom getting shot!"

"Awwww, Jake. You know I can't let you win."

"*Why not?*"

"Because you're twenty-fucking-four. If I can't get your dick hard within half an hour, I'm going to lose my slut card and my woman card! Besides, you know I adore worshiping your hard cock, baby." I trailed my fingertips along my cleavage and smiled.

Jake let out a slight moan as our ride-car moved along.

"Hearing the sounds of the animals makes me want to fuck you on the trails around Animal Kingdom, Jake. There are so many paths to explore. I think we should do that some time very soon, too."

Jake was still looking straight ahead and mumbling to himself. "Baseball... hockey... third-grade teacher... golf."

The fun dinosaur part of the ride ended. Our car moved back into the theater room. Bill and Ellen were back on the movie screen talking about energy again.

"Jake?"

Jake looked at me and I spread my legs and pulled my skirt up showing my bare pussy to him. The panties that I had taken off earlier were dangling from the tip of my finger as I held them out in front of me.

"*Fuck,*" Jake blurted out, then quickly turned his attention back to the film.

I pulled the top of my dress down and exposed my breasts.

"Jake, my nipples are so sensitive right now. I'm really not trying to turn you on with this, but I really need to massage them. It always feels so nice when you do it. Would you like to help?"

"*No!*"

I slid my hand between my legs and began fingering my pussy.

"You should look at me, Jake. I just can't help being naughty when I'm with you. I'm fingering my pussy right now, Jake. It's wet and ready for you. Don't you want to watch?"

"*No!*"

"Jake? If you win, do you want to slide inside and feel how wet it is, or, maybe you would like another hole? Maybe you'd like every hole?"

I saw Jake's dick twitch and he took another deep breath. He focused on the film and only looked forward (I guarantee he had no idea what he was watching). I admired his determination. I never really expected him to do so well. He certainly had his eye on the prize.

"Jake?"

Jake growled and quickly glanced at me again. I stroked my pussy more and spread my legs further apart, but Jake refocused on the movie again.

I pulled my fingers from my pussy and slid closer to Jake. I put my hand in front of his face making sure not to touch him in any way. My fingers were glistening with my wetness.

"See how ready I am for you, Jake? Would you like to taste?"

Jake continued to keep his eyes forward, but I could tell he was close to breaking. I could hardly imagine what nasty things he was thinking about to keep his dick soft at this time. Even I was hurting from being so aroused. Part of me wanted him to win. I wanted him in all three holes! Especially since he was about to burst. It was sure to be an amazing, hard fuck once he got his hands on me. But I just couldn't resist teasing him mercilessly.

I pulled my fingers back from his face and gently sucked them into my mouth.

"Mmmm. I taste delicious, Jake."

I made some light sucking sounds near his ear as I licked each finger clean.

The closing scene started. Alex Trebec and his porn mustache reappeared, hosting Jeopardy with Ellen and Jamie Lee Curtis as contestants.

I moved in closer to Jake and leaned near him to whisper, "I bet Jamie Lee Curtis is a freak in bed. I'd love for her to bend me over and fuck me from behind with a strap-on while I suck your cock and you watch."

I looked down at his crotch to check his reaction. My long red hair fell forward across his lap and the ends kissed lightly across the tip of his exposed dick. It twitched up again from the sudden stimulation.

"Fuck it!" yelled Jake.

He grabbed hold of me by the hair and forced his tongue into my throat. His hand quickly moved my hand to his exposed cock, which was already pulsing and starting to drip. I thought he was going to take me right there in the ride-car during the last moments of the film. Even if it was only a few quick pumps, after this long of a build up, we both needed it. His fingers slipped between my legs and probed inside of me.

Suddenly, our ride-car started to rotate.

"It's almost over. Stop. Stop," I panted.

Jake leaned back from me and rushed to close up his jeans. He struggled trying to shove his raging hard-on back in and zip up. I worked my tits back into my dress and lowered my skirt.

Once the lights came on and we were free to exit, Jake nearly leapt out of the ride vehicle. He took hold of my wrist and roughly dragged me out behind him. We were moving at a near-run pace to the exit of the ride. I knew exactly where we were headed.

"Off to your beloved companion restrooms, Jake?"

Jake grunted.

"Ooooh. You sound like a sexy caveman now. I love when

you're inspired."

"Be careful what you ask for."

We quickly flew past the attraction wait times billboard.

"Imagination is still only a five minute wait, Jake. Wanna go?"

Jake looked back at me as he continued dragging me along at such a rushed pace that I nearly tripped over my own feet.

He grunted again. "Time to pay up on the bet."

"That sounds great! I'm glad that you're so eager to have me cum all over your face!"

"Oh no. You're paying up! I'm taking every fucking hole."

"But your dick got hard! You lost!"

"Your hair touched me... my dick."

"That doesn't count! I wasn't trying to touch you!"

"Sorry. Rules are rules. I hope you're still dripping wet."

"How about a compromise? A truce? Let's call it a draw?"

"What does that mean?"

"I get to ride your face and you get to choose your holes. We both get what we want."

"Deal!"

Jake flung open the door to the companion restroom. We both went in quickly and he locked the door behind us. I wasted no time in sliding my hands under his shirt. His chest was so smooth and hard. I wanted to devour him. He helped me as we both pulled at the fabric to get the shirt off of him.

He grabbed me by the hair and bent me over in front of him and pressed his dick to my lips. I opened my mouth and gladly accepted.

"That's it, you pretty little cocktease. That's hole one!"

After about a minute, I released him from my lips and gave a little tug on his delicious dick with my hand, twirling my wrist around as I let go.

"Get on the floor on your back. It's time to pay up, Mister!"

He didn't protest. He knew we didn't have much time available. If we stopped now, he'd be suffering with blue balls for the rest of the day.

He pulled a poncho from his backpack and tossed it down on the floor. As he was laying down, I balled up his shirt and tucked it under his head. I stood over his face. I placed one leg on each side of his head and hovered over him looking down. I slowly lowered down and felt his tongue probing up, waiting to be buried inside me. I rocked myself back and forth across his face.

"That's it, bitch. Pay up! Make me cum all over your pretty face," I chided as I ground down onto his mouth.

Jake was less than pleased with my unsportsmanlike conduct. He grabbed hold of my hips tighter. I arched back and again my hair dangled down behind me and found his cock. He bucked up as it ever-so-slightly teased over him.

As I rocked back and forth across his face, I could feel my body wanting to cum already. I reached around behind my back and found his cock. I stroked it in rhythm with the movement of my hips riding his face. It felt so swollen and hard in my hand, and I wanted it to fill me now.

"I need to fuck your cock, Jake! I need to fuck it now!"

I released his cock from my grip. I lifted myself up and off his face then slid right back down onto his dick. It didn't take long before I was bouncing hard and starting to cum. Jake reached up and put his hand over my mouth to keep the echo from my moans down.

As soon as I came, Jake bucked his hips up at me and motioned for me to get off.

I stood up and started to straighten myself up. I lowered my dress and ran my hands through my hair.

"Where do you think you're going? I still have one hole left and I intend to use it and fill it with cum... now!"

"We don't have time, Jake. Come on."

Jake grabbed me by the hair and pulled me over to the sink. He bent me over it, tossed up the back of my dress, and pressed his hands into my ass cheeks to pull them apart. After my hard ride on him, his cock was slick and nearly dripping from my wetness. He met little resistance from my unused hole as he entered. I grabbed hold of the sides of the sink and braced myself for a hardcore, fast, ass-fucking, and that's exactly what he delivered.

Within a few strokes, he was pumping his hot seed into me.

Jake backed away and pulled up his pants.

He breathed a long, slow, exhale. "There, *now* the bets are all paid off."

He pulled me to an upright position and guided me so my back was to the wall, then he kissed me. It was gentle and soft, exactly the opposite of how he had just fucked my ass. I enjoyed tasting myself on his soft lips. As he kissed me, his hand slid into my dress pocket. He slowly pulled out the pair of panties that I had taken off earlier.

"Wear these," he said. "You can have them on the rest of the day. They'll help with all the hot cum I just shot up into your ass. I like having you cum-soaked while we stroll around the park."

"You are such a dirty boy, Jake. I adore it!"

I slipped them on and Jake opened the door. We were greeted by a blast of bright sunshine.

I rubbed my butt for a moment in reference to my now-sore ass. "I may resist tempting you with more challenges in the future, Jake."

"Don't be silly. That was far better than a nap."

The Sultan and Harem

Morocco, Epcot

SULTAN'S COLADA
Drink Stand, Morocco, Epcot

2 oz. Rum
1 oz. Almond Liqueur
3 oz. Pineapple Juice
1.5 oz. Coco Lopez or Creme de Coconut
Blend with Ice

I HEARD A KNOCK at my apartment door. When I answered it, there stood a delivery man holding a very large box with 'fragile' stickers all over it. Once it was inside, I was beyond curious to open it and completely bewildered as to what it could be. As the cardboard fell away I peeled the packing material back and noticed a few small, green sprigs.

"*He didn't!*" I yelled into an empty room.

I eagerly pulled at the packaging until the contents were fully revealed. It was a beautiful, delicate, bonsai. I noticed there was a cleanly-typed note; obviously the florist had printed it.

It read:

Hello my lovely red-headed geisha,

I will arrive at Walt Disney World tomorrow afternoon for a weekend trip. I'll pick you up at 5. I'm feeling like Moroccan.

Please accept this bonsai as a reminder of our last adventure in Japan. I couldn't resist sending it to you. Don't worry about killing it. I've made sure that it will be safe in your hands.

Michael

"Son of a bitch! I told him I kill every plant!"

I gently removed the bonsai from the box and placed it on the dining room table. Sitting in the bottom of the box was a book: *How to Care for Your Bonsai*. Attached to the book was another note:

Dear Miss Carson,

I'm available for you anytime, day or night. I'll call regularly to check on the bonsai.

Ken

There was a business card stapled to Ken's note. Along with his name and contact information, the card also had a picture of Mickey Mouse on it. I looked closer at his title, and rubbed my eyes when I read it: *Director, Walt Disney World Horticulture/Resort Enhancement.*

"Well, I guess that should help," I mumbled to myself, trying not to be shocked by all of this. "Michael strikes again!"

I spent a few moments staring back and forth between the beautiful plant, the gardening book, and Ken's card. Then, the rest of Michael's note finally sunk in.

"He's coming tomorrow!"

Michael was always full of surprises. He enjoyed having control over everything. I was convinced that was why he had such success in business. I'd known him for over two years now. We spoke often while he travelled for work. He had an intense personality and high expectations. He oversaw every aspect of his pharmaceutical company. Nobody got anything past him, but this time, I was determined to surprise him.

I didn't sleep well that night because I was excited about Michael's visit. It had only been a few months since I had seen him last. He was a very wealthy man, and it showed in everything he did. His previous visit was the first time that we had been at Walt Disney World together. I haven't looked at the Japan pavilion in Epcot the same way since. I had no doubt that Morocco was about to go onto the magical memory list, as well.

That evening, I dressed and sat ready at the door by five o'clock waiting for him. I could not contain my excitement, and he didn't even get a chance to knock on the door before I had it flung wide open. Michael had the distinct honor of being the only man who had been able to completely charm me and fluster me. I never got used to it, but I secretly hoped that his talent in that area wouldn't go away.

He took one step into the apartment and I was already flushed as he wasted no time in pressing me to the wall, taking my face in his hands, and kissing me gently. In addition to being the only man to make me giggle and blush like a schoolgirl, he was the only man who caused my panties to become soaked instantly.

"I missed you," he whispered into my ear.

I nodded in response and tried to gather myself together as best as I could. He lifted my face up to look at him and smiled. He knew exactly what he did to me.

"Are you ready for a night in Morocco?"

I was ready for our next adventure together and coyly whispered, "Yes, my Sultan."

"Hmmm. Sultan? I like the sound of that. Does that mean that you'd like to have a repeat of our Japan experience, and embrace the culture of Morocco tonight?"

"Yes! I can't wait!"

As we left my apartment, I noticed Michael's driver waiting in the car outside. His driver doubled as his bodyguard, and seeing him reminded me that during Michael's last visit, we were followed by him everywhere we went. There were obvious perks to spending time with a wealthy man. However, it also came with a downside and I despised the lack of privacy.

I curled up next to Michael in the backseat of the car. I had faith that soon we would be so immersed in Disney magic that I would forget about the spying eyes. I rested my head on his chest. Everything always felt perfect when I was in that spot.

The drive to Epcot was not exceptionally long. Michael stroked his fingers through my hair and kissed me softly. His hand slid under my dress and I instinctively spread my legs. As much as I wanted Michael right then, I didn't want to ruin the opportunity for park "fun" that night by having a quickie in the backseat of the car. I caught him by the wrist and held him back. Michael did not appreciate that. He probably had not been told "no" to anything in years!

"Are you trying to tease me, my dear?"

"No Michael. It's just that... I have a surprise for you later."

"This must be some surprise."

His hand wandered up the inside of my thigh. Again, I grabbed his wrist to stop it. I kissed him deeply in an attempt to distract him.

"I promise to make it up to you later, Sultan."

We arrived at the backstage entrance of Epcot, near Test Track, just as we did during Michael's last visit. He never waited in lines or used the main entrance.

"A girl could get used to this VIP treatment, you know?"

"A girl should if she's with me."

We exited the car and walked into Epcot through the back of the Morocco pavilion. As usual, his bodyguard followed us.

"Michael? What is his name?"

"Yasha."

"Well, if Yasha is going to follow us around again, shouldn't he be in something more appropriate for a theme park? The black slacks and black t-shirt are odd in Florida."

"What do you suggest?"

"Something more touristy!"

"Do you want him to wear a shirt with a Dole whip or turkey leg on it? Or worse, one that says, 'I'm with Dopey'?"

"Those would all be great with the right set of Mickey ears."

Michael looked at me with a stern look of disapproval. Yasha heard the entire discussion, but gave no reaction; he wasn't even cracking a smile. Even at Walt Disney World, it was all just business as usual for him.

We moved along through the paths of Morocco and entered into a clothing shop. Several racks of shirts and gowns lined the walls. An exotic-looking Moroccan Cast Member with stunning dark eyes approached us.

"May I help you?" she questioned.

"What do you have in men's clothing?"

"Right over here. Everything is made in Morocco, all cotton. It's very hot there, too."

She led us to a small rack of clothing and held up a pair of light-cream colored pants with a bit of "Hammer-pants" shape to them. She then pulled out a pale-yellow shirt and held it up with the pants.

"Well, Michael, it's not a turkey leg t-shirt, but this should work."

I took the outfit from her and pulled out a similar pair of pants and another shirt in pale-blue, then handed them both to Michael.

"You're kidding?" he asked hesitantly.

"Nope."

"Both of us?"

"Yes, please. We're embracing the culture, remember? We could always go to Mouse Gear and pick up some matching 'I'm with Dopey', 'I'm with Grumpy' shirts for the two of you if you'd prefer? But I think you would look much more handsome in this."

Michael took the clothing and went with Yasha to change. It delighted me that he had decided to be a good sport about our Moroccan adventure.

After a few minutes, I heard a very bubbly voice outside the door of the shop saying "hello" and greeting Guests. I got excited. I had been expecting that voice and the girl who went with it. I looked up at the door and in walked a slim, bright-faced blonde. It was Holly, and she was all smiles and bounce as usual!

"Holly! You made it!"

She raced over to me and gave me a big hug and kisses all over my cheeks. I could tell that she was bursting at the seams to tell me about her new advancement.

"How's the new position treating you?"

"*I love it!* It's like a dream come true! You know I've always wanted to be a princess! I mean... Cinderella? She is *the* princess! Her castle is *here*! I'm Cinderella! I don't think I'll ever get over the excitement!"

"Well, I always did say that one day you would be a princess here. I'm sure that everyone at The Great Movie Ride misses you though, especially during the Last Ride of the Night."

She giggled at me, but our conversation was cut short by Michael and Yasha returning. Yasha stayed near the front entrance of the store, but Michael walked towards us.

"Michael, this is Holly. She used to work at The Great Movie Ride. She recently became a princess here."

"Wow. Congratulations, Holly. Let me guess. Cinderella?"

"*Yesssssss*!! It's so great! I work at the Akershus restaurant in Norway."

"I let Holly know that we would be here today and she agreed to join us for dinner. Surprise!"

Michael smiled. "Of course. What a lovely surprise, too!"

Holly reached over to a display table in the shop and picked up a fez. She quickly went up onto her tip toes, reached up to the top of Michael's head, and placed it on him.

"There. Now your outfit is complete. Plus, you look like Abu. Everyone loves Abu," Holly said with a glowing smile.

Michael looked at me. "Abu? The monkey?"

"Sultan Abu," I said.

"I can live with that," Michael said, nodding.

Michael offered us each an arm and we exited the store.

We wandered around some more listening to Holly's tales of being a real-life princess at Walt Disney World. Her bright eyes twinkled and she glowed as she spoke. She loved being a princess and skipped from store to store giggling about her new experiences. Eventually, we broke away from the shopping and made our way to the museum at the front of the pavilion.

"Moroccan Style: The Art of Personal Adornment," Holly read off of the sign above the entrance. "I *love* this room."

We walked inside and a burst of air-conditioning engulfed

us as we all let out a contented moan. It was a small room with very ornate tile work and sculpted-molding detailing. There were display cases filled with various clothing from different regions, jewelry, and beautiful designs of henna that decorated the arms of mannequins.

I pointed to the small glass enclosure showcasing the henna art.

"I love this. It's so feminine and beautiful. I go to the henna artist here all the time. She covers half my arm in just a few minutes. It lasts for over a week, too."

"We should get some for you both today," Michael suggested.

Holly started bouncing, making her perky little tits on her petite frame jiggle. "I've never had it done! That would be great, and my costume has long gloves so it will be covered for work!"

"But first we have to find some appropriate clothes for you both."

"*More shopping!*" Holly screamed

Just when I thought Holly couldn't get any more excited, she nearly exploded. We left the air-conditioned comfort of the museum and followed the paths back into the pavilion again to the furthest shop in the back. Moroccan music filled the air. It was almost too loud but still seemed appropriate. The shop was filled in every corner with clothes, trinkets, jewelry, and even tiles with intricate geometric designs.

Holly went straight for the belly dancer designs. The skirts were long fringe with rows of jingling coins that wrapped around the hips. The matching top was more like a crisscrossed scarf that left her belly exposed. Coins dangled from it as well.

A Cast Member smiled at us from the other side of the clothing rack. "These are very popular."

"What fun costumes. How could any girl resist them? Do they have a special name?" I asked.

"Yes, bedleh. It means... suit."

"Bedleh? Suit? That's a simple description for such elaborate clothing. Holly, which bedleh do you like?"

"This!" Holly held up a deep-blue colored outfit.

I could tell it would look stunning on her.

I noticed a gown that was displayed on a mannequin. It was a sleek long design, almost like a robe. It was a pale blue that nearly matched the shade of Michael's shirt. It had a wide, sparkling, silver border that accented the front and around the ends of the sleeves. A wide band of silver cinched in the center of the gown at the waist. It was like the Moroccan version of a kimono.

"Michael, it reminds me of our night in Japan," I said as I caressed the fabric.

"Perfect," he said, smiling.

Holly and I both dressed. While I admired my gown in a mirror, I heard loud laughter behind me. I turned and saw one of the Moroccan Cast Members dancing in the middle of the store. She was wearing one of the coin-covered hip scarves. She was smiling and waving her arms as she twirled her hips. She danced like a professional belly dancer and Guests crowded around her. She took the hands of Guests to encourage them to join her. Some jumped in eagerly, while some just shook their hips for a moment, then ran away blushing. Then, she took Holly's hand. Holly happily danced around the room like a natural. She made great use of the new outfit and swirled her hips around, elated at the sounds of the jingling coins.

I felt Michael's arm run up along my back. We both watched Holly dance in her new, flowing bedleh. Her movements were the opposite of what one might expect from a proper Disney princess. The curve of her back arched deeply as she raised her arms into the air and shimmied her body. Holly bit lightly on her own lip, and I thought back to how soft her lips felt when I kissed Jake's cum off of them in The Great Movie Ride.

"Do you like your surprise, Sultan?"

"Yes, very much. Thank you."

We both continued to watch Holly and the Cast Member dance as the crowd grew bigger around them.

"Every Sultan needs a harem," I said. "This is a start at least."

Michael adjusted his fez. Holly and the Cast Member stopped dancing and Holly rushed over to us.

"Thank you for the clothes, Michael."

She reached up towards him, put her arms around his neck, and gave him a big closed-mouth kiss on the lips then released him and did the same to me.

I took her hand and we walked back out towards the front of the pavilion dressed in our glorious new clothes. I've had henna done so many times in Morocco that the artist immediately recognized me.

"You look gorgeous! So, good to see you again! Getting some henna today?"

"Yes, both of us are," I said, pulling Holly over closer to me.

"What design would you like?"

She had a book of designs to choose from. I looked at Michael for his approval on a design.

"Like the displays inside the museum," he said.

"That would be beautiful. A design to cover the entire hand and arm is traditional. It will be lovely with your new clothing," the artist said.

Holly and I sat at the henna booth talking about all kinds of girlie things as if we were at the nail salon. Michael and Yasha went to the walk-up drink stand and enjoyed a beer while they waited.

"This is insane," Holly said. "He's *really* cute and really rich!"

I laughed. "Yes, he is both. Wait until we go to dinner after this. I don't know exactly what will happen, but I am *certain* that it will be over the top. It's just how he lives. It's all normal to him. Just take deep breaths and try not to squeal *too* much."

Holly only nodded in response as she eyed them at the bar. The artist completed the henna on both of our hands and arms in less than twenty minutes. We were very careful not to touch anything as she instructed. It was good that we were going to dinner so that we could sit and let it dry without disturbing it too much.

"All ready, ladies? Dinner awaits."

Michael bowed slightly as we walked past him in our elegant Moroccan outfits with freshly henna-decorated arms and hands. The sun was starting to go down and there was about an hour until *Illuminations* would begin.

We arrived at the entrance of Restaurant Marrakesh in the far back corner of the pavilion. It was surprisingly quiet and there were no strollers parked outside of the restaurant. It was eerie how quiet it was in the dimly-lit alley; I could even hear the water flowing from the fountain that sat in the right corner outside of the restaurant. I instantly knew that Michael had already set this up to be special.

We walked in and the waiting area was lined with Moroccan Cast Members welcoming us into the restaurant. When we stepped inside, it was more beautiful than ever. I had dined there before. It looked like a banquet hall in a palace. It was decorated with amazing tile work and intricate designs in every corner with support pillars throughout the room. Unlike the last time I had dined there, all of the tables and chairs that usually filled the center of the restaurant had been removed and only one table remained. Surrounding it in the room were large, decorative lanterns perched on top of five-foot high pedestals.

Holly started to let out a squeal. I reached over and covered her mouth gently.

"I tried to warn you."

We sat down at the table and a handsome dark-skinned Moroccan man with penetrating eyes asked us what we would like to drink.

"The Sultan's Colada, please," said Michael.

Holly and I both started to giggle.

"The ladies would like the sangria."

"Yes, sir."

Michael was sitting across from me. He looked as handsome as ever in his cool cotton shirt that peeked open a bit on the top. Holly was sitting next to me and holding my hand under the table. She looked around at everything like a wide-eyed child. She usually wasn't shy, but Michael had the same effect on her as he did on me.

Once the sangria arrived, Holly chugged back her first glass before I barely had a sip. Within a few minutes, a second glass of sangria arrived for her and she drank half of that as well.

"You keep that up tonight Holly, and Cinderella is gonna lose her shoes again!" I laughed.

Holly and I had naughty fun together before, but it had been with guys closer to her age. Michael was an entirely different world, it was understandable that she was nervous. I felt the same way. A mere wink from him and I blushed.

We ordered our food and as the sangria kicked in, Holly relaxed and was able to join in on the conversation again. While we were eating, Moroccan musicians sat in the center of the room and played for us. The palace-like room, the beautiful music, feeling gorgeous in our new clothing, and dining in the soft glow of the lantern light all made it magical. Michael had done it again. He was as generous and charming as he was handsome. I certainly was happy to be a part of his harem.

As we finished dinner, the music pace picked up and a belly-dancer entered the room. She was stunning. She had long, wavy, dark hair, caramel skin, and big, beautiful, almond-shaped dark eyes. She was wearing an ivory-colored skirt and top that were completely covered in crystals. Her midriff was bare allowing the light from the lanterns to twinkle off the crystals as well as her skin. She slowly and seductively gyrated and danced around the room.

After the first song, she approached us, reached out her hands, and invited us to join her in the open dance floor. Holly did not delay in jumping up. I followed her. The dancer slowly showed us her controlled hip movements, then had us try it with her. The music picked up pace again and we danced around happily. I'm certain that the sangria helped!

Holly and I joined hands and danced closer to each other as the song went on. The belly dancer circled around us with her crystal-coated skirt twirling up into the air. Holly turned her back to me and leaned against me as we swayed our hips in unison and looked right at Michael. It was obvious that he enjoyed the entertainment. He leaned back in his chair, smiling in true sultan fashion.

I reached my arms around the front of Holly and placed my henna-decorated hands over her breasts. The coins hanging off of her costume jingled on her hips, making a deliciously enticing sound. I kissed her neck as I closed my eyes and held her close to me. She leaned back further into my arms as we danced.

Within a few moments, I felt a strong hand reach up through the back of my hair. It quickly got my attention. I released my lips from Holly's neck and saw Michael standing in front of us.

"Let's go," he said.

The music continued to play as we dashed out of the restaurant. I turned towards a side door in the back alley to exit the pavilion towards the car, but Michael pulled me in a different direction. Holly followed along as we went to a small nook in the corner near the restaurant entrance. It was off to the side near a small water fountain and a cement bench. I always wondered if Guests ever noticed this quiet spot, even during the busiest part of the day.

An entrance to a shop sat further down the path from us, but it was closed for the night. Yasha stood in the middle of the walkway as a lookout towards the path to the other side of the restaurant.

Michael walked backwards to the wall and pulled us both

towards him. The music from *Illuminations* began as Michael leaned down to kiss me. I felt Holly's hands slip down the front of my gown and I helped her pull it down to reveal my tits. I heard the light jingles from her outfit as they played along with the *Illuminations* music. She licked at my nipples and sucked them each into her mouth. Michael held my head back. I pulled at the waist of his pants and put my hand in to stroke him while he watched her work on my tits.

We all knew that we only had about fifteen minutes until *Illuminations* ended and the Guests scattered everywhere. Yasha would have had his work cut out for him to ensure our privacy if that happened.

I pulled Holly's face up from my breasts and shoved my tongue down her throat. Her lips were so small and soft compared to Michael's. I could have kissed her all night. I reached my hand up under her jingling skirt and teased her with a finger. She was soaking wet and so was I. I pulled my hand up to my mouth and licked my finger, then put it into her mouth too. She sucked at it eagerly.

"Holly, lie down on the bench," instructed Michael.

She moved out of the corner and laid down with her head at the end of the bench. Her legs spread wide with one foot on the ground on either side of the bench. Michael stood behind me and lifted my skirt while we walked towards her. He led me forward until I stood straddling the bench...and her face. I lowered my body. My knees were barely bent as Holly raised her face up to meet me and buried her tongue deep in my pussy.

"*Fuckkkkk!*" I moaned out loudly.

The blasts of fireworks and music from *Illuminations* drowned out my voice. Michael moved along side of us and watched as I ground down onto Holly's face. He wasted no time in pulling his new Moroccan pants down and bending me forward to put his dick in my mouth. I slid back and forth on Holly's face at the same pace as I sucked his cock.

Michael looked at my mouth on his cock and Holly's wet pussy spread on the bench. He reached down and started finger-fucking her. Her toes curled up and I felt the vibration of her moans in my pussy. He slid his finger out of her, pulled his cock out of my mouth, then replaced it with his soaked finger. I sucked it until he pushed my head down into her pussy.

Holly mumbled under my hips as I sucked at her swollen pussy lips and rubbed my fingers over her clit. Every time she moaned or attempted to speak I fought back an orgasm. I looked at Michael with a desperate gaze. He had seen that look in my eyes many times. He knew that I was about to cum.

He moved behind me, pushed my dress up further, and grabbed both of my hips. I instinctively arched my back for him as I felt his dick rub along the lips of my pussy and towards Holly's mouth. Her tongue licked me and lapped at his cock when he pressed it in between us. I continued to finger Holly and cup my entire hand over her pussy lips. The more I rubbed, the more she moaned and vibrated her mouth around my clit and Michael's dick.

Michael pulled back slightly from my wet pussy and Holly's face. I felt him tease the entrance of my ass with the head of his dick. He knew that with her tongue in my pussy and her lips pressed to my clit that if he penetrated my ass I would cum immediately. He loved to feel that tight hole around his thick cock. But even more, he loved to force orgasms from me when he chose. Just like in business, with fucking he also wanted full control.

I felt him push the tip harder against my ass. It started to slowly slide in. I moaned and licked at Holly's pussy while I pushed back and filled myself with his cock inch by inch. Once he was buried balls-deep in my ass, I knew it wouldn't be long until I flooded my cum all over Holly's face.

I rocked my ass back on his dick and teased my pussy along her probing tongue. Holly reached up and tightly gripped onto my thighs while I opened her wide with one hand and used my other hand to mercilessly rub her clit. She was screaming under me and Michael started pumping harder.

I heard the finale of the *Illuminations* fireworks. Explosion after explosion went off high in the sky as our secluded dark alley lit up. Holly's legs kicked up into the air and she started cumming. Her hips lifted off of the bench. Cum squirted out of her in a big arch that nearly reached the fountain next to us. As the last fireworks exploded, Michael grabbed me by the hair, pulled me back towards him, and pumped his hot cum inside my ass.

We all took a few seconds to slow our breath then untangled from each other. Michael grabbed Holly and gave her a long, soft kiss to lick my pussy juices from her lips. Even with tangled hair and flushed cheeks she still looked like a beautiful princess.

As we straightened our clothing, we heard the announcer's voice at the end of *Illuminations*:

"Ladies and gentlemen, the entire Epcot family thanks you for having been with us for *Illuminations: Reflections of Earth* presented by… 'semen'."

We all laughed like silly teenagers as we walked towards the backstage exit.

Yasha held the door.

The Wave of the Future
Tomorrowland Transit Authority
and Carousel of Progress

BLUE GLOW-TINI
Resort Shared Drink Menu

2 oz. SKYY Infusions Citrus Vodka
1 oz. Bols Peach Schnapps
1 oz. Bols Blue Curacao
2 oz. Sweet and Sour Mix
1 oz. Pineapple Juice
Serve in a Glass with a Sugared Rim
Add Glow Cube

ID YOU WEAR panties today, like I asked?" said Damon.

"Yes. That was a very odd request coming from *you*, but I was afraid to ask details."

We casually strolled over the bridge towards Tomorrowland after watching the three o'clock parade in the Magic Kingdom, and *this* was the type of conversation that occurred when I was with him. I'd met Damon through a friend. My laptop had crashed and he'd helped me fix it. In the process of making sure that all my files were restored, he'd stumbled upon my folder of naughty selfies. He took the opportunity to compliment my pictures and reveal his fascination for women with large breasts. I took the opportunity to thank him for the help by letting him play with mine.

He wasn't particularly muscular or panty-dropping handsome, but he had pretty eyes. Damon looked like a typical, average, guy. He quickly taught me that looks could be deceiving. The sex was anything but "average". He was one of those geeky guys who loved all things techie. He obsessed over every electronic gadget that he could get his hands on. I was sometimes shocked at how much fun he was in bed and often wondered how he found time to come up with the creative games we played, especially since his nose was always in a computer. Was there an app for that?

As we entered Tomorrowland, I knew he intended to play

another creative sex game. This was the first time that we were taking our adventures into the Disney World parks. I had no idea what he had planned, but at least his sudden question about my panties had distracted me from the demolition of the Swan Boat Dock in the Castle Rose Garden. Although I didn't really remember the Swan Boats from my childhood trips to the Magic Kingdom, I already missed the dock. I'd recently adopted the covered dock as a new quiet place to literally stop and smell the roses. That was not the first time that one of my personal retreat spots at Disney World was transformed. The original Top of the World Lounge in the Contemporary, the Sara Lee Bakery in the Disney Village Marketplace, and the heavily air-conditioned Main Street Cinema in the Magic Kingdom were just some of my quiet hideaways that were now casualties of progress. If I was a paranoid person, I'd have thought there was a conspiracy afoot to systematically steal all of *my* private places.

We entered into Tomorrowland and I didn't even have to ask where he wanted to go. I just walked straight ahead towards the Tomorrowland Transit Authority (TTA). We both loved it because it was one of those classic attractions that held so much nostalgia. It always made me think of Walt. I actually still called it WEDWay, since it was named after Walt's initials, W.E.D. for Walter Elias Disney. I never understood why they'd decided to remove Walt's name from it, though I guess I couldn't really complain about it much. As disrespectful as the name-change was to the attraction, I had violated it in my own way *many* times. Sometimes I wondered if Walt would have been upset by the amount of finger-fucking and blowjobs that occurred on that attraction. I smiled when I thought about it and walked a little faster. I was excited to go do it again!

We reached the TTA and went up the escalator. That thing seemed *so* slow when I was excited and there were people standing in front of me on the way up. I wondered what

Damon had planned though, since he had specifically told me to *wear* panties. Those usually got in the way of the fun. I couldn't wait to find out what that cute little geek had in mind this time.

We boarded the ride-car and the Cast Member in the loading area looked concerned.

"Wow. We've got some excited Guests here today! You know this just goes *through* Space Mountain, right? It's not a rollercoaster."

"Yeah, we know. We're just fans of the classics," Damon responded.

"Well then, please enjoy your ride on the WEDWay PeopleMover and your Grand Circle tour of Tomorrowland."

I smiled ear-to-ear at the Cast Member. "Thank you!"

"I think he just covered the foreplay for you Damon. 'WEDWay PeopleMover Grand Circle tour' sounds like sexy, dirty talk to me. Plus, I love when the Cast Members know their shit."

"It's all a part of my brilliant plan, my pretty."

Damon rubbed his hands together and did his best evil-genius cackle.

The ride started off slowly, my legs bounced excitedly as we went along. I knew the dark part of the ride was coming up soon and Damon would turn it into an E-ticket attraction instantly. We weren't even there yet and I began pulling up my sundress, panties be damned!

We entered into the first dark section of the ride and, as expected, Damon grabbed hold of me and kissed me. Then his hands went straight between my legs.

"Are you sure those were a good idea, Damon?"

"Yes. You'll thank me later."

I felt him push my panties aside and tease me with a finger. Something hard pressed between my pussy lips and I jolted back a bit. He held me tighter, kissing me more and pushing deeper until I felt filled. He pulled my panties back over to cover me and ran his hand up my thigh to the edge of my dress. He pulled it down and straightened the fabric across my lap. His lips stayed pressed to mine while he completed his task.

"What *is* that?" I mumbled through his kiss.

I pulled back from his lips and we were once again outside in the daylight. He reached into his pocket and pulled out a small electronic device.

"What geeky gadget thing did you get now, Damon?"

I squirmed around trying to settle myself and get comfortable with the object inside of me. Damon held up the device. It was a small, black, rectangular plastic box with a dial on the side and a button in the middle. There were some small words on it too, but I didn't look closely enough to read them.

"This is a remote control."

We entered into the next covered area and I heard the recording say, "Space Mountain."

Suddenly, I felt a low, dull pulse vibrating through me and I jerked up.

"*Holy shit!* That's kinda awesome."

He looked at me with a sly smile and held the remote up. I saw his thumb deliberately slide to the dial on the side of the remote. Again, the vibrations and pulses buzzed, this time more furiously. I gasped as my head fell back.

Then they stopped.

I laid back in the ride-car and took a few deep breaths.

"Well, this is sure gonna be quick. That was intense."

Damon started to laugh at me.

"Ohhhh. No. No. No. That would be too easy and not much fun at all. We've got *hours.*"

"You've got to be kidding!"

I was not amused. As much as I appreciated a fun sex game, having my pussy vibrate while inside Space Mountain seemed like more stimulation than I could bear. He knew that I loved the Magic Kingdom. He knew that the classic rides turned me on.

"You're taking advantage of my weakness, Damon."

"Yes."

"You expect me to play along with your torture?"

"Yes."

His hand twitched and the vibrations pulsed through me again on full speed and, once again, I collapsed back in the seat and let out a squeal before they came to a stop.

"Feel good?"

"Yessss. God, yes!"

"Shall. We. Play. A. Game?"

"You are *such* a dork!"

The vibrations kicked on again and my body flailed back and forth in reflex.

"Okay, okay! Whatever you wanna do, Damon! Whatever you want!"

I wriggled around in the seat, took a deep breath, and thought to myself that this could turn out to be my best park visit ever, or, it could ruin me for all future trips. Memories that induced instant screaming orgasms and drew attention from Tomorrowland security were not my life's goal, but, I decided to risk it.

I looked at Damon, smiled sweetly, and licked my lips.

"Let the games begin," I challenged.

As we exited Space Mountain, he showed me the remote. I was able to examine it more closely in the daylight and noticed five settings:

1. Foreplay
2. Tease
3. Pulsation
4. Vibration
5. Climax

The side dial said "Multi-Speed".

Damon took the remote from my hand and turned it to the lowest setting on the dial.

"Let's run some preliminary testing," he said.

"Damn I love it when you geek out, Damon."

We entered the last dark area of the track. It passed through the Buzz Lightyear attraction. Damon put his arm around me and nuzzled his face against my neck.

"Number one: foreplay," he whispered.

I felt a series of long, slow, buzzes with a slight pause in between each. It certainly got my attention and I couldn't help but moan slightly.

"Welcome to *Buzzzzz* Lightyear Space Ranger Spin, my precious!"

"If this didn't feel so damn good, I'd smack you, you twisted fuck."

Damon gave me a peck on the forehead. We pulled out into daylight again as the vibrations halted.

"You love it!" he laughed.

I was sad when we reached the ride exit. I didn't want to leave. I moved very carefully as I stepped out of the car, walking slowly to adjust the toy inside of me.

"Off to Carrousel of Progress, shall we?"

"Sounds good. Sitting until I adjust more with this would be a good thing."

Damon was practically skipping. I was heel-toeing my way along slowly, trying to not let the vibrator fall out of my already dripping-wet pussy.

"You were right. Panties were *definitely* a good choice today. This game could have ended very badly without them. I can just see it now: 'Mommy, why did that lady just lay an egg?'.... Sonofabitch!"

"You're welcome!"

Luckily, everything stayed in place as I walked, and we made it to the Carrousel of Progress. We only waited a minute before the theater opened for us. We went inside and sat in the back. There were less than ten other Guests and they sat front and center, leaving us a private row in the back. The host began her safety spiel, requesting that all Guests must remain seated because the entire theater would move approximately every four-and-a-half minutes. After an additional minute of recorded show announcements, the show began and the theater moved us to the first scene. Damon turned on the vibe as he whispered.

"Let's begin again. Scene one: foreplay."

I relaxed in my seat and enjoyed the delicious stimulation. It was the same setting that he tested on me earlier. The long, slow buzzes felt incredible. I held my legs together to muffle the vibration noise but Damon assured me that he couldn't hear it, so I didn't worry too much.

I loved this attraction. Even as a child, it was one of my favorites. I loved how the ice box and oven doors opened. The banter between the family members amused me. I'd never figured out why the young girl in the first scene never appeared in the rest of the attraction. But this time, I wasn't paying much attention to the details. The vibrations distracted me, along with Damon's groping hands down my dress. I felt like we were two teenagers in the back of a dark movie theater.

The first scene ended and the attraction theme song started to play as the entire theater moved again. Damon blasted the vibrator speed to high and began to sing along with the loud music.

"It's a great, big, beautiful, tomorrow...."

I gripped onto the arms of the seat. I felt like I was already on the edge of cumming. As the theater movement and music stopped, he turned the remote dial back down to low.

"Scene two: tease," he whispered.

The vibration pattern changed. Now it did a series of quick pulses: a low, slow buzz, another quick series of pulses, then a more powerful buzz. This was most definitely a *tease*. I bit onto my lip and leaned forward in the seat as my pussy clenched around the toy. I had no control over it. Damon grabbed me by the hair and pulled me back to sit up in the seat.

"I'm gonna cum. I'm trying not to scream," I said, breathlessly desperate.

The theater started to move and again Damon sang along. The vibrations went up to high. My body shook as it forced an orgasm from me. I let out a deep breath but somehow, managed to not scream. If I had, I think Damon would have sang louder and acted as if I was singing too... like an alley cat in heat!

As our seats stopped in the next scene of the attraction, I felt the vibrations slow inside me. I expected them to stop, but Damon had other plans.

"Scene three: pulsation."

"There's *more?*" I whimpered.

I looked at him with wide eyes as the toy inside me changed patterns again. He just smiled. The pulses were amazing. They were quick-paced and felt like a strong tongue was lapping up through my pussy lips. I began grinding down in the seat and I stared at Damon as I imagined that I was riding his face while he tongue-fucked me.

I became caught up in the moment and hardly noticed that the theater was moving again. He happily sang along with the theme song, bouncing his head back and forth and tapping his feet as the pulses went up to high and I nearly exploded. If we were alone, I would have torn his clothes off and fucked him into the damn floor. Damn, I adored that fucking freak!

The theater settled in to the last scene of the show.

"Viiiiii *-brationnn,*" Damon said in a sing-song voice.

The pulses stopped. Instead, the whole toy began to vibrate. It was so intense that everything from my clit to my ass vibrated… hard! There was no stopping the orgasms at this point. My breathing quickened. He knew exactly what he was doing to me. He reached his arm around my shoulders, covered my mouth with his hand, and pulled my head into his chest. My body was shaking with one orgasm after another.

I knew the Carrousel of Progress show well. Even with

my eyes closed, I knew that the last scene showed outdated technology, tacky sweaters, and a burnt turkey. For the first time, this was my favorite part of the show. Even as fake smoke drifted through the theater, I was blissfully unaware. The entire attraction could have burnt down around me, and I would not have noticed or cared. I think there may have been more smoke coming off of me than the damn bird!

One final time, the theater started to move. The vibrations between my legs stopped, but my pussy was still pulsing. I could barely catch my breath. I needed a fucking drink.

"Why did you do this to me in a dry park?"

"Come on. I'll get you a Mickey bar."

I could barely walk out of the theater. My knees trembled. I felt weak, but in a good way. Damon held on to my arm as we headed towards the Lunching Pad for a seat. He slid the chair under me as I collapsed and rested my head on the table.

"I'm gonna sleep right here. Go on without me. I'll be fine."

"You just need something sweet to perk you up. I'll be right back."

He wandered off as I just lay there. I heard someone come over and ask if I was okay. I never looked up. I just mumbled something incoherent and gave a thumbs up.

Soon, Damon came back and I felt something cold touch the side of my cheek. I opened my eyes and saw him standing there, smiling, holding Mickey ice cream bars.

"This should do the trick."

He pulled me upright and handed me my ice cream bar. I managed to remove the wrapper, and sucked on Mickey's cold chocolate ear. I was orgasm-drunk and numb, floating in a happy place. It felt pretty good.

"You know, we only did four out of five settings."

"What?"

"You still have one left. I never put it on climax."

I didn't speak. I bit off Mickey's ice cream ear.

Damon took the remote out of his pocket and placed it

onto the table in front of us. I stared at it and felt my body start to wake up. It was really a fun toy and I was curious, very curious.

His hand hovered out over the remote, taunting me. My pulse quickened. My chest raised and lowered rapidly with anticipation. Then... he pushed the button.

A strong wave of vibration shot through me. It was even more intense than the vibration mode from before that sent me into uncontrollable orgasms inside the Carrousel of Progress. Then suddenly, it shifted to the strong tongue-fucking pulses. Back and forth from vibrations to tongue, it teased and tortured me.

"*Oh my fucking God, Damon!*"

I threw my head back and gripped onto the table, slamming my Mickey bar down! Ice cream and chocolate bits flew everywhere and my body shuddered as a wave of orgasms washed over me again.

After a few seconds, I recovered and opened my eyes. All over the table were bits of mangled Mickey bar. A jaw-dropped Cast Member stood staring at me about twenty feet away. I smiled at him and blew a kiss. He never moved; he didn't even blink.

I straightened my dress and wiped off a spot of chocolate shrapnel.

"Feeling better?"

"Much!"

I reached over to Damon and took his Mickey bar.

"So, where ya wanna cum next ?"

"This toy might actually improve Stitch," I joked.

"You're asking a lot. How about Space Mountain? This time I'd like to hear you scream."

An Adventurer's Life is Best
Adventurers Club, Pleasure Island

KUNGALOOSH, SINCE 2000
Adventurers Club, Pleasure Island, Downtown Disney

2 oz. Daily's Strawberry Daiquiri Mix
2 oz. Orange Juice
3/4 oz. Captain Morgan's Spiced Rum
3/4 oz. Light Rum
1/2 oz. Blackberry Brandy
Blended with Ice

*Y*EP, IT'S GONE," I said.

Jake and I stood at the entrance to Pleasure Island in Downtown Disney where the old train car ticket booths still sit abandoned. We stared up at where the last Pleasure Island sign had been mounted above the small bridge.

"I heard they took it down yesterday," responded Jake.

"Once they closed the clubs, especially the Adventurers Club, I guess it didn't really matter anymore. The old neon Jessica Rabbit sign where she kicked her leg back and forth… that one is something to mourn. That should still be hanging *somewhere* on Disney World property!" I said.

"Yeah, you showed me pictures of that one. It was hot. Who doesn't want to see sexy Jessica on their vacation? This place needs more of her everywhere!"

We wandered over the small bridge, past Raglan Road Pub. Their house band played outside. A handful of Guests sat there intently listening and sipping on Guinness. There were still great things to enjoy here, despite the changes happening.

We continued walking along the path that went uphill through Pleasure Island where the clubs used to be. It was all under construction for the new Disney Springs project, and most of the old clubs were already torn down or earmarked for other projects. If anyone held out hope for a return of the nightclubs to the old Pleasure Island, it was lost now.

The energy that pulsed through the area was amazing when Pleasure Island was in its original form. Music and dancers kept everyone hyped up. During the day, it was a quiet place with simple shops, but at night it came to life! I just hoped that the nighttime entertainment for Disney Springs didn't turn in to another infamous dance party with twenty-two-minute versions of techno-mix Sherman Brothers' songs. I saw hints of that happening in the Marketplace area on weekends and during special events on the Westside. Hopefully Pleasure Island would be spared a similar fate. For now, live musicians regularly performed in several locations throughout the entire Downtown Disney area. It was a small consolation prize for the entertainment that once was there, but, at least it was something. I've never witnessed a bad live music performance there. But there was not enough booze in Downtown Disney to make me tolerate constant dance-party ambiance.

"This really was a great place to have some special Disney memories and express yourself in more *adult* ways. I was lucky enough to just be coming of age when the Pleasure Island clubs opened. It's a real shame that you weren't even born yet, Jake."

"Well, I guess you can just teach me all about it, Princess."

"I'm trying, Jake. You're an excellent student, by the way. You're a natural when it comes to naughtiness. You know, Pleasure Island is where *I* first learned."

"What do you mean?" he replied.

"This," I waved my hands around motioning to the whole area surrounding us. "This is where I lost my Disney virginity." I smirked.

"Hahaha. That's awesome!"

I pointed to the closed-up Adventurers Club sitting off to the right side of the walkway, "More specifically, my naughtiness began... *there*."

We walked past the club and took a seat on some long couches that were located at the top of the hill near where the

Pleasure Island Stage and Neon Armadillo Club (later BET Soundstage) once sat. Jake pulled me close and put his arm up around me. I rested my hand on his inner thigh and my head on his chest.

"So this is where it all started, huh? Tell me every little slutty detail," Jake said.

"Hoping to pick up some tips for later?"

"You know it, Princess."

"Okay. Picture this," I pointed around to the various areas of the island.

"Imagine a big, open stage over here to the right with a live band. Dancers with big hair and sexy outfits did hot routines on stage. I can still remember a girl riding on a guy's back as he crawled across the stage. Along the street were a few big electronic screens. They constantly flipped between images of the Pleasure Island logo and shots of the band with the dancers. The streets were usually packed. The Guests all laughed and danced around in the street as they held their drinks. There was a big decorated kettle in front of the Adventurers Club that looked like something out of Jungle Cruise. A Cast Member in a safari outfit served drinks out of the kettle as naughty nurses showing lots of cleavage walked around in short skirts carrying faux-syringe shots. That was my first dose of adult Disney: seeing those ladies walking around! It was like the Disney version of Mardi Gras.

"One of the best things about Pleasure Island was that every night they would bring in the New Year. They did a countdown with the stage dancers and band leading it. Then *bam*! The fireworks went off. Confetti shot out of cannons all over the Island. I'm talking enough confetti to coat everyone and everything. I have no idea how they cleaned it all up each night. Then the dancers jumped down off the stage and danced up and down the hill. They joined with the Guests to create a massive conga line that went back and forth and up and down the street. That was all just the stuff out on the open streets!

Inside the clubs, especially the Adventurers Club, was where the real show happened."

"Wow! Massive street party with booze and naughty nurses? Sweet! No wonder everyone is so pissed that it's not around anymore. Sounds like a great time," said Jake.

"It really is a shame. The outside activity was just the foreplay. Inside the clubs was where the action happened. Inside Mannequins Club, they had a revolving dance floor, and above the dance floor was an area where hot dancers kept everyone pumped up. Watching them made it feel more like a concert than a club because the performances were very theatrical. Everyone wanted to dance instead of just sit back and relax. It wasn't a quiet place. It also had great catwalk areas upstairs to explore. I guarantee those dark corners saw lots of fucking."

"Did you fuck on the catwalks?"

"Surprisingly, no. I enjoyed Mannequins, but my favorite spot was the Adventurers Club. I was obsessed with it before I even realized there was a huge cult-following for it. The Adventurers Club didn't have such dark, private corners, but that place was so sexually charged that it was nearly impossible to get out of there without being excited. There were characters who mingled with the Guests and did shows, too. The French maid was very risqué: she was in heels, a short skirt, and ruffled panties that revealed themselves when she dusted around the room. She sat in laps, was very flirty, and bent over a lot. And, you know how bold I am when I talk, Jake?"

"Oh yeah. It's hot."

"Well, she was pretty bold, too. Everything she said was a blatant sexual innuendo. I even remember a show where the song that she sang had lyrics about her wanting Indiana Jones to grab her, kiss her, and whip her!"

"Seriously? At a Disney club?" Jake said, shocked.

"Yesss! And the interactive animatronic, Goddess Babylonia, she was outrageous. Well, she was a Goddess, I suppose? She was a big, cracked, ancient, statue-style face that hung over a doorway in the club. She could see Guests and talk to them. She always harassed people sitting at the bar near her. She made men get on their knees, bow, and worship her. It was hysterical. Every direction you turned had entertainment. Their signature drink, the Kungaloosh, was badass. It was so strong and really delicious."

"So, are you gonna tell me you got drunk and got it on with the maid?"

"No, but close. The butler."

"Butler?"

"Yes. He greeted Guests inside the entrance that was right there." I pointed over to the empty club again. "That door led to the upstairs level of the club. There were two floors inside. Every room was filled to the brim with stuff. Each item was *supposedly* a unique collectable gathered on an adventure by the club and Pleasure Island owner Merriweather Adam Pleasure. A lot of the relics and photos in the upstairs level even had hand-typed tags on them describing what they were. The level of detail was insane."

"Was he a real guy or was he created by Imagineer storytelling?" asked Jake.

"Jake, you are a Cast Member. You should know by now that nothing at Walt Disney World is real. Every detailed description in the place was total bullshit."

Jake smiled and nodded.

I continued. "The inside of the club looked like something out of a mansion. There was a beautiful, winding, staircase that led down to the lower level. The main room had a bar with stools and some antique-looking couches and chairs. Babylonia hung over the doorway towards the bathrooms. The Colonel, another interactive animatronic, sat in sort of a balcony seat overlooking the main parlor. There was also a silly moose. He was funny because he was supposedly sent to the upholsterer instead of the taxidermist, so he had tassels hanging off of him.

"Then there were side rooms. They were more like nooks actually. They had no doors. There was wraparound bench seating that lined the walls for maybe twenty Guests to sit. The one small side room was the mask room, and there were shows with the interactive tribal looking masks that hung on the walls. The other small side room had a floating genie head in a box. He was interactive with the crowd too. Both rooms were dark and intimate when there was no show going on in them."

"Now we're talking!"

"No Jake, not yet. I didn't defile the entire club. Of course, I should have once I heard it was about to close. It would have been purely out of love and nostalgia, of course!"

"Of course," Jake said, chuckling.

"The bar area and two small rooms only made up half of the downstairs level of the club. The main shows were in a big library, and they changed those shows a lot. There was a Balderdash Competition, a Radio Show, the Maid Show... all kinds of stuff. Most of the shows had singing and comedy and tons of crowd interaction. You could spend all evening going from show to show in the different rooms and interacting with the characters and animatronics. That's actually what most people did. The other clubs faded away because there was no reason to leave the Adventurers Club once you entered."

Jake looked up at the clouds, pondering. "There's nothing like that now. I can't really think of any place here where Guests can go to have that type of interactive, constantly changing entertainment experience for a full evening."

"Exactly, Jake. It really never got old or boring. It was an immersive, adaptive improv show from the time that you walked in the door until it closed each night. As much as I tell you about it, it's nearly impossible to describe. I heard about it before my first visit but, I truly had no idea what to expect until I went and saw for myself.

"The week that my special adventure happened there, I was on my college summer break. I was your age. I went to the club four nights that week. The first night, I was curious. I was still a good girl then, and I loved to just tease the boys in school."

"You *still* do that!" Jake quickly interjected.

"Hahaha, well, yes, but now I have more plans for after I tease them thoroughly, as you've experienced firsthand."

"Mmmmhhhmmm."

"But I wasn't as bold and outgoing then; I was still young. So my first night at the club, I mostly kept to myself and watched. I spent a lot of time looking at the special adventurer finds upstairs and reading the hand-typed tags on the items. I honestly thought a lot of it was real at first! Most people didn't stick around upstairs for long because the shows were downstairs. I liked the quiet there. It was a break from all the action going on outside.

Since the butler stayed upstairs a lot, he and I interacted quite a bit. He always stayed in character. He'd walk around in his formal uniform and gloves with his hands clasped behind him, and stand at attention when he spoke to me. He would hover around me when I looked at the artifacts and act suspicious. One time, he informed me that there was no need for me to contemplate stealing anything because there were a dozen undercover armed guards ready to swoop in at a moment's notice to bring swift justice upon anyone who disturbed the collection.

Another time, he approached me and said that sometimes they took suspicious Guests into a back room and interrogated them to make sure they were not after the prized artifacts of the club. Of course, I told him that I'd pay extra for *that* show. I remember that I winked at him and he actually stammered for a moment. I wasn't sure if the reaction was from the character, or sincere from the man who played him. That was the first time that I realized how much fun it was to express myself and be bold towards a man. His reaction was all the encouragement that I needed to come out of my shell.

I spent a lot of time the first two nights making my presence known to the butler. For my second visit that week, my outfit was more revealing and I spent more time in the upstairs area practicing the art of teasing with the butler. I liked to lean over the balcony and pretend that I was looking down on all the Guest and Cast Member interactions in the main room below. I'd arch my back and let my skirt ride up my hips, each time a little bit further. If he approached me, I would flirt unapologetically. I taunted him. I'd tell him that he should be more worried about fetching a drink for me and doing his job as a proper butler than wandering around aimlessly on the upper floor. He even bowed to me and apologized. It was really hard to tell if he was enjoying it or if he was just doing his job and was extremely irritated by my teasing him."

"He was enjoying it," said Jake.

"Well thank you, darlin'." I leaned in and gave Jake a long deep kiss.

I continued the story. "On my third visit for the week, I actually went back to watching some more of the shows downstairs instead of playing around upstairs with the butler. I ordered my Kungaloosh at the bar and wandered from room to room as the shows in the small side rooms happened.

At one point, I was waiting in the main room for the official Adventurers Club new member induction ceremony and I realized just how naughty the club was. I was seated in a chair facing towards the bar. The bar stools lowered and raised by a button that the bartender could push from behind the bar. I saw this guy sitting next to a girl at the bar. He was hitting on her like crazy. Nothing terrible; it almost seemed like they knew each other. I got the strong impression that they were both Cast Members from the club because they looked slightly familiar. Well, when the guy started getting more pushy towards the girl, the bartender actually raised up the girl's stool and then lowered down the guy's stool. He was put in his place down on the floor and was basically talking to her knees. It was pretty funny until he leaned forward and put his face in her crotch. He only did it for a second, but I saw it plain as day. She kicked him and slapped him dead on across the face. They had to have been friends though because they both started laughing. I was still shocked. I never expected to see that in an open bar area anywhere at Disney, even in a nightclub. Nearly everything done in that club was a bit naughty. I loved it.

The official member induction ceremony started soon after the barstool incident that night. It was basically another show. It took place in the main bar. Of course, every Guest there wanted to participate. They all crowded into the room as it began."

"Oh, Jake! Jake, you need to learn the club song!"

"I have to sing for you to keep telling me the story and teasing me?"

"Yes you do. Now, play along please."

"Yes, Princess."

"It goes like this....
Marching along we're adventurers.
Singing the song of adventurers
Up or down
North, South, East, or West
An Adventurer's life is best!
Kungaloosh!"

Jake repeated after me less-than-enthusiastically while sitting out in the open. He was so adorable when he was cranky.

"*Kungaloosh, Jake!*

"Anyway, after the new member ceremony was over, we were all invited into the library for the next show. The whole crowd began to move inch by inch around the furniture in the room towards the library doors. The butler appeared to help encourage members to be courteous of other members while selecting seats inside the library.

I didn't rush to jump ahead of the crowd. Instead I lingered near the bottom of the spiral staircase and waited for the room to clear. Once I began to make my way across the room to the library, I took the opportunity to brush past the butler and make sure that he felt my breasts slowly rub against him. He looked down at me. I smiled up to him and whispered, "Excuse me."

I followed the group of nearly a hundred people as we slowly transitioned from one location to the next. I wasn't in a hurry and ended up at the back of the pack. Just as I reached the doors, I felt a tug on my arm. I turned my head. It was the butler. I ignored him. He pulled my arm again. I didn't even look at him. He stepped up behind me and grabbed my left wrist with his left hand, and I felt his hot breath on the back of my neck.

'I'm going to have to ask you to remain here madam,' he whispered next to my ear so that nobody else could hear him.

I wasn't sure what was going on, but I stayed there and stopped trying to move into the library with the rest of the crowd for the next show.

'You *like* to tease,' he whispered while still breathing down the back of my neck.

I could feel chills run down over my body.

'What?' I responded, shocked.

'You *like* to *tease*,' he said more boldly.

I lowered my head and looked at the floor. I felt a blush go over my face.

'You tease, I *take*,' he growled into my ear.

My legs began to tremble. I thought this as odd for his character. I felt slightly embarrassed, but I was strangely aroused by his comments. I decided to play along. I was curious.

He gripped my wrist tighter and led me towards the doorway where Babylonia hung above the opening. As we passed under her into the hallway, I heard Babylonia mumble, 'Looks like somebody was naughty and got in trouble!'

I didn't know what was happening or where he was taking me. I still wondered if it was part of the interactive show. We rounded the corner and the butler pushed the button on the elevator. I was upset. I thought that I was being escorted out of the club. I didn't think that my flirting was that inappropriate based on a lot of the things that I saw happening in the club. He said he was taking me. I didn't understand. I was confused but still curious.

The elevator doors opened and he directed me to go inside. He followed me in, hit the button, and quickly pinned me face-first to the back wall of the elevator.

'Wha..?' I gasped as he held me in place.

'I don't like being teased. If you tease, I *take*.'

He placed his hand on my back to hold me to the wall, then turned to push a button on the control panel. The elevator stopped. I felt his warm body press against my back again. He held onto both of my wrists with his hands. I could feel the chill on my cheek as my skin rested against the cold elevator wall.

He whispered, 'You like this, don't you?'

I tensed up. I didn't answer. He pressed harder against me. I let out a breathy, 'Yes.'

He whispered more softly, 'You like to be taken.'

'Yes.'

He ground his hips against my ass. 'You like to feel a hard cock against you.'

I stopped responding. I was trembling and trying to catch my breath. I just kept thinking how I wanted all of these things. I wanted them deep down, but I couldn't say it. I couldn't admit that I really wanted that to happen. Not here. Not at Disney!

He tightened his grip on my wrists. His breath was so hot on my skin. He put his lips to the back of my neck.

He whispered again, 'You like a hard cock against you.'

I felt my will break as I closed my eyes and softly responded, 'Yes.'

'Tell me again.'

I moaned out quickly, 'Yesss.'

'You want to do everything that I say.'

'Yes!'

'You want to fulfill my every desire.'

'Yes.'

'You want me to make your fantasies come true.'

'God, yesss... pleaseee.'

His hands released my wrists. They trailed up over my arms, through my long hair, and down over my body.

'You want to feel me inside you... right... here.'

'Yesss.'

He brushed his lips across the back of my neck and I reached my hands back to touch him, any part of him, just to feel him and know it was real.

'You want me to fuck you.'

'*Yes*,' I pleaded.

I pressed my hips back against him. He guided my head to the side and exposed my neck. He slid his gloved hand up and down my neck.

'You want me to taste you.'

I moaned, 'Yessss.'

His lips pressed to my neck, and then teeth sunk down into me. I reached back for him and he pressed my hands back up to the wall. I was in such pain aching for him and wanting it to happen. I was so wet, so excited. I couldn't wait for him to fill me.

'You like to tease.'

'Yes.' I smiled slightly and almost giggled.

He grabbed me by the hair, forcefully pulling me down to

the elevator floor and onto my back. It all happened so fast. Suddenly, he was between my legs. My short skirt had already slid up to my waist from him rubbing against me while I was pinned to the wall. He traced my smooth, shaven cunt with his finger. As I pressed my hips up towards him, he grabbed my nipple hard. I gasped, arched up, then dropped my hips back down.

'You like to tease.'

'Yes... yes... please,' I said as I slid my hips back and forth, wanting him.

He opened his pants and pulled out what I wanted. It was what he made me admit that I wanted. It was what he had seduced me into saying. I wanted him to fulfill my dirty fantasy. I hated him for making me want it so much, but I needed it.

I felt the tip of his hard cock go inside me. I began to moan and he pulled it back out.

'You like to tease.'

'Yes,' I said. 'Yesssss.'

He ran the tip up and down me again.

'You like to tease.'

I screamed, 'Yesss!'

He put his gloved hand down over my mouth to muffle my sounds as he thrust into me. I heard people laughing and talking outside the elevator. I was terrified that we would get caught, but he just smiled. He kept his hand over my mouth and slowly fucked me. Every move was deliberate and controlled. I tried to press back up against him, but he pushed his hips onto me. He kept me pinned while he circled and stroked his dick down into me.

The sounds of the people outside faded and his pace quickened. I felt like I was in a dream as my body began to shudder.

He whispered, "Cum for me."

I responded with the only word that I knew at that moment:

the word he taught me that night.

'Yessssss!'

Jake leaned down and kissed me.

"That was fuckin' hot, Princess. I'm so glad that he turned you into a Disney slut."

I chuckled. "You know what else, Jake?"

"Hmm?"

"The next night I went back to the club, and he did it *again!*"

Jake smiled at me with an evil look. I could see that his dick was rock-hard. I took him by the hand and tugged on him to stand up and follow me over to the closed-off entrance to the Adventurers Club. There were a few plants positioned as a barricade to the stairs in front of the door. I looked towards the club longingly and sighed.

Jake took my face in his hands and kissed me.

He stared deeply into my eyes. "If they ever open that club up again, Princess, I'm fucking you in it."

"Jake, if they ever open it up again, I'm fucking *you* in it."

He smiled and kissed me again.

"Let's go, Princess. We don't want to be late for the luau."

The Luau
Polynesian Resort

LAPU LAPU
Polynesian Resort

2 oz. Myer's Original Dark Rum
2 oz. Pineapple Juice
3 oz. Orange Juice
1 oz. Sweet and Sour Mix
Serve in a Pineapple Over Ice
Float with 1 oz. Bacardi 151

I'M SO EXCITED, Jake!"

"You crack me up," he said, laughing, as we pulled away from the guard shack at the entrance to the Polynesian Resort parking lot.

"I haven't seen the Luau since I was a little girl. I hardly remember anything about it. I know there were pretty hula-girls that reminded me of the dolls inside of Small World, and muscular men dancing around with no shirts, and a fly landing in my rice while we ate outside so I couldn't eat any more of it."

"Ha! So, you've always been a picky princess then?"

"It was a dirty fly! Ewww!"

We got out of the car and walked up to the Great Ceremonial House. It was the main entrance to the resort. It housed the check-in area, shops, restaurants, lounge, and a two-story iconic waterfall that had adorned the lobby for over forty years. Unfortunately, the resort was undergoing major refurbishments. Rumors floated around that the waterfall was scheduled to be removed during the project, but I never dreamed they were true. It was a tropical-themed resort, so how could it not have a waterfall covered in lush, overgrown foliage? I was shocked when the automatic doors opened and we were greeted by huge wrap-around walls that enclosed the entire area where the fountain once stood.

"What the fuck?" said Jake. "They weren't kidding."

"I don't want to talk about it!" I said sternly. I looked down at the floor as I walked as fast as I could out of the back of the Great Ceremonial House towards the Luau Cove.

I took long, deep breaths during the brief walk. I tried to convince myself that the resort would still be lovely with a new design. I was determined to have a fantastic time at the Luau. We checked-in at Luau Cove. We were given leis and took our seats relatively close to the stage, left of center. I adjusted my leis and noticed the nylon flowers were frayed around the edges and little pieces of thread were shedding all over my clothing. There was a label on the leis.

"Jake, the leis say 'Made in China'. The last time that I was here, they gave out real shell necklaces. I still have several of them on display in a glass jar with my Disney souvenirs. They sure do change a lot of stuff around here."

"It will be okay, Princess. Wine is included with dinner."

"You always know the right thing to say, Jake."

Less than a minute later, our server arrived for our drink order. The food arrived shortly after. It wasn't like what I remembered, but not much was at the Polynesian Resort that night. We still enjoyed watching it. It was a quirky story and reminded me of a community theater production, but it was a lot of fun. I had just started my third glass of wine when our server informed us that it was last call, so I ordered a fourth. Jake reached under the table and petted my thigh when the server stepped away.

"Four glasses, Princess? Wine goes straight to your head. This is gonna be a fun night with you."

"Mmmmmmhmmmm."

I groped Jake back under the table, and gave him a small kiss on his neck. I rested my head on his shoulder. He was right about the wine: after seeing the construction in the resort lobby, the wine made the evening much better. Being with Jake also made the evening much better. He was always so much fun to hang out with at Disney. He was a great "friend with benefits", and the sexiest Cast Member to ever hit on me in the parks. The fact that he was a handsome, muscle bound, tattooed, twenty-something didn't hurt either. I'd never had a bad adventure with him, so I knew that our luau date night would be no exception.

In typical Disney fashion, the luau included an audience participation scene of the show. The performers invited any Guests who wanted to learn the hula to join them in front of the stage. I stood up, drank back the last of glass number three, took Jake by the hand, and pulled him up with me to join the fun.

All of the dancers in the show were extremely attractive. As I stood at the stage, a caramel-skinned buff dancer danced right in front of me to demonstrate the proper hula dancing movements. He stared right into my eyes the entire time that he danced. I think I was smiling and flirting back, but I may have actually just been giving him some crazy-looking drunk face. Nonetheless, the liquid courage must have kicked in as we headed back to our seats because as I passed by the dancer I whispered to him.

"I'll be at the pool bar later."

He paused for a moment, looked at me, and smiled. Without saying a word, he ran back up on stage. I walked back to the table. Jake was already there. He was cranky and made grouchy faces at me for having forced him to wiggle his ass in front of a crowd of strangers.

"That was embarrassing. Don't make me do that again... ever."

"Relax, Jake. You've got a cute ass. You should wiggle it more often. Oh, and by the way, we might have company tonight at the pool bar."

"What did you do now? You were only gone for two minutes!"

"But... but... *look* at him, Jake! He's all bumpy with muscles!"

I looked at Jake with a pleading puppy dog face, then followed it with a huge, cheesy, tipsy smile.

"Well, since you and the other two girls gave me that awesome birthday surprise in The Great Movie Ride, I guess I owe you a big thank you."

"Yes. And you're very welcome. But he probably won't show anyway."

"Ha! Have you *met* you? He'll be there."

"You think?"

"Definitely. I'd put money on it."

I kissed Jake on the nose and sat back to watch the rest of the show. The last act of the luau was more like what I remembered as a kid. There were hula dancers with pretty outfits, muscular men doing fast-paced dances, and even "The Chief" twirling fire batons all over the place. He was incredible!

The funniest part of the show was that the topless muscular male dancers came out first, and when they started to perform, some of the women in the audience were clapping and whistling. A few of the ladies who felt the need to whistle may have had a bit too much wine with their dinner as well. However, the reaction was very different when the gorgeous, half-naked, hula girls flipped their hips around and wiggled their cute little asses. I expected some of the same reaction from the men that the tipsy female Guests had. They must have been terrified to reveal that they enjoyed watching the beautiful women. The men all remained totally straight-faced and quiet. They all had the same looks on their faces as the men who circle around the belly dancer at the Morocco pavilion in Epcot. As if to say, "I'm not supposed to be watching this, but I like watching this, but I can't let my wife see me liking this, but all the other men are watching this, so I guess I'll just sit here and watch it, but I'm afraid to smile, or blink, or look directly at my wife." This was usually accompanied by the facial expression of a confused puppy wondering if he was allowed to jump up onto the couch.

Not Jake, though; he was all smiles and may have even had a bit of drool on his chin. He stared at the pretty girls and thoroughly enjoyed watching them wiggle their hips.

"This is so hot. Why haven't I come here before?"

"I agree, Jake. It's a very inspirational performance."

I reached my hand under the table, across his lap, and rested it in his crotch. As I trailed my hand slowly up and down his inner thigh, I felt a familiar, hard bulge in his pants. He looked over at me and shook his head slowly back and forth.

"I can't take you anywhere, you naughty little drunken slut."

I laid my head back onto Jake's shoulder and left my hand to rest on his thigh for the remainder of the show. The luau came to an end with a very peppy Elvis-in-Hawaii style finale. I thought it was very entertaining. The food was good. The wine was good. The dancers were hot. I was tipsy. The evening was turning out better than I had expected.

"That was fun, Jake. Thank you for taking me."

"You're welcome, but you still have to put out. You know that, right?"

"Of course."

We exited the show and wandered around the resort. It really felt like a tropical paradise with palm trees and white sand beaches. We eventually ended up at my family's traditional relaxing spot: the patio near the pool bar. Despite having had a few glasses of wine with dinner, it was a tradition that we must enjoy Lapu Lapu drinks on the beach when we were at the Polynesian Resort. The Lapu Lapu drink was almost as legendary as the water fountain in the Great Ceremonial House lobby. It was an exceptionally boozy drink with lots of rum and juice. The best part was that it was served in a big pineapple. It was the perfect nightcap, and in a perfect world I could have sat on that beach and slowly sipped on one every night of my life!

We sat at one of the tables near the big volcano pool and

looked out over the water towards the Magic Kingdom. I remembered when I could see the top half of the castle from there. Now the trees were grown up and just the top turrets peeked out. The Polynesian Resort beach was still one of the best places to relax in all of Walt Disney World.

That night, as we enjoyed our Lapu Lapu, I showed Jake one of the great secrets of sitting at that location along the beach. Even a lot of the Guests who stayed at the resort didn't know about the *Electrical Water Pageant*.

"See the boats, Jake? They're moving along out there in the water in the dark. You can kind of see the outline of the square structure that sticks up out of each boat. That part is what lights up during the show."

"Yep, I see them. I've never watched the show before."

"The *Water Pageant* has played around Bay Lake since 1971. It's a real tradition. They better not think of cutting this out too to save a buck! It's awesome to see how excited Guests get when they are out here at the pool and don't realize that it's going to happen. The floats suddenly light up out on the water and it's like an instant sprinkle of surprise pixie dust."

The music started up and screens of light bulbs lit up in different colors that created a sea serpent, dinosaur, and leaping dolphins. The show only lasted a few minutes, but I still enjoyed it like when I was a child.

"So what did you think, Jake?"

"That was great. I didn't know what to expect when you told me about it."

"I'm so happy you liked it. I saw it so many times as a kid that I started to look for burnt-out bulbs on the screens. I always wondered if they would get replaced by the next night or still be burnt out. I still can't help but look for burnt out bulbs."

We strolled along the beach after the show. Each time we came across a dark corner, we made out for a minute, just kissing and groping each other. I always enjoyed those hidden, playful, moments with Jake.

"We should head back to the pool, Princess. We need more Lapu Lapus. Then we can watch *Wishes* fireworks over the Magic Kingdom. It will be romantic to get you in the mood."

"You know *Wishes* doesn't get me in the mood Jake. I miss the old *Fantasy in the Sky* show. It had all that great, themed, music from the attractions! *Wishes* just doesn't compare. Plus, the *Wishes* music is so depressing. It sounds like the children singing it are so sad. It makes me want to swan dive off the castle."

"Would you wear Tinkerbell's flight outfit as you did that?"

"Shut it, Jake."

"It would be really *hot*!"

"There's something wrong with you."

"Yes, my dick is always hard."

"No, that part I actually really, really like!"

Jake took my hand and led me back towards the pool as I continued to babble about *Wishes* and the old pool at the Polynesian prior to the huge volcano. I sat down at the tables between the beach and the pool again and Jake ordered more Lapu Lapus. By the time that *Wishes* ended, I realized that I'd spent more time staring down into the boozy pineapple than watching the fireworks. I did, however, catch myself singing along with the music a few times. Damn Disney and their catchy music!

After the fireworks ended, Jake ordered another Lapu Lapu for us to share. We were very relaxed from the other drinks, but decided on one more as the pool bar closed. Most Guests cleared out of the pool and beach area. There were a few stragglers, but not many. It was quiet enough that two ducks wandered up to the pool and got in the shallow end of the water. They just floated there. It looked like they were warming up in the heated pool. I think they were basically "going to bed". A woman walked over to try to touch them and they swam around in circles, annoyed. She gave up quickly and the ducks settled back down in their place in the shallow end.

I was distracted watching the ducks when I suddenly felt a hand run along my shoulder and down my arm. I turned quickly to see that it was the dancer from the show, *and* he'd brought a friend: the fire-dancing Chief!

"Heyyyyy, you made it!"

"Of course."

He leaned over and gave me a small kiss on each cheek. Then the Chief moved closer to me and did the same. They both totally ignored that Jake was even there.

I was all smiles and looked over at Jake. He rolled his eyes at me, tossed the pink umbrella out of the Lapu Lapu, and took a swig of it straight out of the pineapple without using a straw. I guessed that was his silent expression of protest. It would not have surprised me if he bit off the side of the pineapple and challenged the dancers to an arm-wrestling match. Silly boys.

"I hope you had a great second show. I really enjoyed ours. I hadn't seen it since I was a little girl. My name is Blu, by the way. This is Jake."

Jake casually lifted his hand in a half-wave acknowledgement.

"I'm Moe, short for Mortimer."

"That's cool! Just like Walt's original name for Mickey."

"Yep, the same."

"Everyone calls me Curly," said the fire dancer. "Because of my hair."

"Because he constantly fusses with his hair like a girl," Moe interjected.

I paused for a moment and thought about their names. Then I started to laugh.

"So, you guys are Moe and Curly? Hahahahaha!" I looked at Jake and nudged him on the arm. "Too bad you aren't a Larry! I'd do all three of you together just to be able to say I nailed Larry, Moe, and Curly in one night!"

As soon as the words left my mouth, I wanted to suck them

back in. My drunk voice had taken over. I'd been Lapu Lapu'd and all the filters were gone. My drunk laugh quickly turned to a nervous laugh.

"Umm... that was just a joke."

Moe winked at me and started looking me up and down.

"Was it?"

I sunk down into my chair and pulled over the Lapu Lapu from Jake.

"So, what do you guys bench?" Jake asked.

After that, the rest of the conversation became a blur. It was like Charlie Brown's teacher started talking and I only heard random words that stood out. Mwa wa wa waaa waaa gym. Mwa waaa mwaaa waa waaa protein. Mwaa waa waa waaa waaa gym.

I stared out at the water towards the Magic Kingdom and the Contemporary Resort. It was so quiet out there at night. The Guests had totally cleared out, the ducks were curled up sleeping next to the pool, and I was enjoying an *excellent* Lapu Lapu buzz and loving the world. Moe reached over the table and ran his hand up and down my arm.

"Getting sleepy, pretty girl?"

"Yeah a little bit."

"Princess needs a nap?" Jake said mockingly.

Moe stood up and took one of my hands. Curly did the same with my other hand.

"There's a great napping spot down the beach here," said Moe. "We think you'll really like it. It has a nice view over the water, too. Come on."

They each tugged my hands, so I stood up and followed along with them. Jake picked up his pineapple, which probably only had a few sips remaining, and trailed behind. I giggled a lot as we walked. The luau guys became very touch feely. They touched my arms, my neck, and my long hair. I put my hands up under Moe's shirt and leaned against him as we walked. He felt so good. I wanted to kiss every inch of his bronze chest.

"Come over here, Princess."

Moe and Curly led me off the path and down to the beach where there was a secluded hammock swaying gently in the breeze. I sat down on the edge of it with my feet dangling off the side. They both stood next to me and held me steady as I swayed back and forth in it gently.

"Ooooh, this could be fun," I said.

Moe didn't waste much time. He tilted me back across the hammock, pulled down the top of my dress, and fondled my tits. Curly followed his lead. I heard Jake's voice coming from a slight distance away.

"She likes it when you pinch her nipples."

Jake spoke in an uninterested and bothered tone. I turned my head slightly and saw him sitting down on the sand a few feet away, watching us and crunching on ice from his empty Lapu Lapu.

Moe moved to the other side of the hammock. My attention was quickly brought back to him when he leaned down to kiss me. I closed my eyes and swayed. I enjoyed the feeling of their hands and mouths all over me. They lifted my dress and explored every inch of my body as I dangled across the hammock.

Moe quickly, but gently, grabbed my hair up tightly by the scruff of my neck and explored my mouth with his tongue. He moved to my neck and bit down into my flesh. As he continued to suck and lick my neck, he reached out and gripped tightly onto my tits. I started to moan and hardly noticed that Curly had pulled my legs up into the air.

"Slap her clit. It makes her dripping wet."

Jake called out more helpful tips in his catty, mocking tone, but I paid him little attention. Curly took Jake's advice and slapped my pussy repeatedly. Each time I felt his hand, I jumped and squirmed around, causing the hammock to swing back and forth. I pulled my legs free from his grip and wrapped them around him, giving him an open invitation.

Moe trailed his tongue up from my neck and into my mouth again then quickly replaced it with his dick. I arched up while my long red hair brushed back and forth against the sand at his feet. I was expecting to be throat-fucked since it was actually a fantastic angle to slide deeply. But he had other desires.

"These are so nice," Moe groaned under his breath, as he continued to manhandle my huge breasts.

He pulled his dick from my hungry lips and slid the soaking wet shaft between my tits. My neck arched back more. I practically did a backbend off the hammock while he gripped one breast in each hand and pulled me back and forth. With each long stroke, he buried his dick in deep. I lifted my head slightly from under him to press my lips to his balls. I licked and sucked gently. They had already tensed up.

As the hammock swayed, Curly gripped onto my ass with my legs still wrapped around him, and mounted me onto his dick. I was dripping wet and he slid right in to the hilt. They gently rocked the hammock back and forth. Curly slid deeply into my wet cunt while Moe straddled my face and fucked my tits. I felt like a pleasure see-saw at the playground.

At the same time, both of them quickened the pace. Jake teased again from the sidelines while he watched the action unfold.

"Fuck her good, guys. The little slut loves cock more than anything."

Within two strokes of Jake's comments, Moe and Curly both shot cum all over me and my dress. I dangled like a rag doll over the hammock when they were done. Jake walked over to us and dismissed them both.

"Thanks guys. I'll take it from here. You can leave."

Jake reached out his hand to each of them as if to tag off and the dancers walked away smiling. Jake had fucked me enough to know that I was not fully satisfied by them. He leaned down towards my face and kissed my forehead.

"Looks like you had fun. Does my princess want more?"

Between the wine, Lapu Lapus, and two Polynesian dancers, I didn't have the energy to respond. I just looked at him and smiled.

He pulled me up from the hammock, steadied me on my feet, then pulled the cum-soaked dress up over my head and tossed it back onto the hammock. He took my face in his hands and kissed me deeply. He knew how to make me purr with pleasure. We lowered onto the ground together and he quickly entered me. His body felt perfect against me. He pumped into me hard and deep. He knew how to make me cum quickly. I arched up and began to moan and cum as he pressed his lips to mine to muffle the sounds.

We lay tangled up on the sand for a few minutes while we listened to the water lap up onto the edge of the beach.

"Jake?"

"Yes, Princess?"

"I hate sand."

The Promotion
Walt Disney World Railroad, Monorail

MONORAIL PINK
Top of the World Lounge, Contemporary Resort

1 1/4 oz. Gin
1 1/4 oz. Pineapple Juice
1 1/4 oz. Orange Juice
1 oz. Grenadine
1/2 oz. Lemon Bar Mix
1 1/2 oz. Heavy Cream
Blend with Ice

NOTHING WARMED ME inside on a cold day like spending time on Main Street at the Magic Kingdom. It was where my earliest memories of Walt Disney World magic began. Still, I missed the old Main Street Cinema where I once sat on the oddly-placed steps in the middle of the room and watched the small movie screens that showed classic Disney animation. It had been a wonderful place to enjoy quiet and air-conditioning on a hot June afternoon.

The Magic Shop was also a special treat to visit as a kid. One year, I finally saved up enough allowance and bought the classic linking metal rings that magicians always used in their acts. I wanted to know what the special trick was that made them work. Two steps out of the store, I had them out of the box and found out the answer. I was so disappointed to see one of them had an open side. I honestly thought there was some real "magic" involved in that trick.

The place that I missed the most on Main Street was the Penny Arcade. Even with all those rides and characters all over the park, the Arcade was a special place that I most looked forward to seeing. I loved the machines that cost a penny to turn the crank and see a picture-flip style movie play. My favorite movie showed a young schoolboy who got into trouble. The teacher spanked him with a ruler while he was bent over the desk. I felt naughty when I watched it. I saved my pennies all year for that one and snuck into the Arcade to see it as much as I could. I thought that someone would catch me and I would be in trouble because it made me feel so excited. I guess I've always been a little bit freaky.

Those places are all gone now. They've been transformed into souvenir shops. I've stopped into the old Cinema (that is now an art shop) and stared at the side walls from time to time. The structure still remained where the small movie screens once sat. It was good to see that hints of those places still existed because I really did miss all of those great things.

Even with all of the changes, there was nothing like the feeling of walking around on Main Street in the Magic Kingdom. The music, the view of the castle, the sounds from the train, the smells from the Ice Cream Parlor and Confectionary all made me feel wonderful. They helped me get lost in a happy bliss.

I was enjoying one of those happy, blissful days on a chilly afternoon in January. I lingered in the Confectionary to take in the smell of recently made cotton candy and rice krispy treats. Even when I felt chilled on the outside, the magic of Main Street warmed me on the inside. Sometimes a Cast Member would hand me a big pile of fresh, sugary, cotton-candy fluff wrapped in wax paper. It was the most delicious thing when it was still warm; there was nothing like it. But that day, nobody was making fresh cotton candy. The sweet scented air had teased me. I must have just missed it.

I found myself staring at a large display of lollipops to compensate for the lack of fresh, warm, sugar fluff. The lollipops weren't as big as I remembered as a little girl, but they were still fun. Big swirls of colored sugar always made me happy, regardless of my age. I was particularly fond of the long twisted ones that looked like a unicorn horn.

I created a new hobby with unicorn lollipops for when I was bored. My inspiration came from a man who stumbled off the curb in front of the Emporium because he was so distracted by watching me suck on one. Since that day, I occasionally wander through the Magic Kingdom with one in my mouth and make a point to smile at any man who seemed grumpy. It always surprises me how it makes grown men blush. They get a cheap thrill and I get an instant cure for boredom. Playing with the tourists has always been fun.

As tempting as it was, that day I decided to skip the sugar and just browse, so I left the shop without any treats. I took my time window shopping as I made my way down Main Street towards the castle.

About half-way down Main Street, there was a small side alley. There was rarely a soul there. I often sat at one of the small bistro tables on the sidewalk and watched the Guests all rushing around out on the street. There were fantastic Imagineering details in that alley. My favorite was the music lessons that were taught upstairs. If I listened closely, I could hear the sounds of singing or a piano playing. The upstairs window even had an advertisement for the music lessons. Additions like that fascinated me.

As I turned down the alley, I heard someone behind me. I didn't pay it much attention other than to be slightly irritated that someone was attempting to invade my quiet corner. I arrived at a small table, and I was about to sit down when he spoke to me.

"Hi, I'm Bill."

"Hello, Bill. May I help you? Are you lost?"

"Not exactly. I just wanted to give you this."

He reached out his hand towards me. He held a small Disney gift bag with a wooden stick poking up out of it. I hesitated and he placed the bag onto the bistro table, then took a step back. My curiosity got the best of me and I peeked inside. It was one of the unicorn lollipops that I had paused to admire in the Confectionary.

"I saw you looking at it in the candy store. I think you should have it."

"I'm pretty sure that it's a bad idea to accept candy from strangers."

He looked at me with a big, toothy, almost-nervous grin and extended out his hand to offer a handshake. I reached up slowly. He eagerly grabbed at my hand and gave it a good, hearty shake.

"Well, like I said, I'm Bill. So, I'm not a stranger anymore!"

"Umm, okay, Bill. Well in that case, nice to meet you. I'm Blu."

I noticed he had a plastic name badge clipped onto the pocket of his shirt. Sure enough, it said Bill. I motioned towards his badge.

"Here on business... Bill?"

He quickly pulled off the badge and clumsily attempted to force it into his jacket pocket. It made me giggle to see him so flustered. Although I had no plans of teasing the tourists today, since one had come to me, I took it as a sign. I overheard him mumbling to himself once his name tag finally made it into the pocket.

"Smooth, Bill, real smooth," he said.

"Why don't you have a seat here with me?"

I lifted my foot under the table and put it on the chair across from me to push it out. Bill's cheeks turned slightly pink. He became more nervous than I had expected. It was quite endearing; he was adorable. While Bill sat down, I removed the lollipop from the bag and peeled at the plastic that encased it.

"So, what type of business conference brings you here, and, do you follow girls down alleys often?

"Oh, goodness, no! I just... I dunno. I'm here for a conference. I do computer stuff. My boss wanted me to come here with him. I just do what he says. It's been a really boring week sitting in the conference rooms. We finally came here to the park today. He's off riding rollercoasters, but those make me sick. I've been walking around. Then I saw a pretty girl with red hair cross my path in the candy store and I... well, ya know."

"Yeah, I know. I guess there's a reason why they all shout 'we want the redhead' in the pirates ride, huh?"

Bill nodded quickly. I finally managed to remove the plastic off of the entire unicorn lollipop. I leaned in across the small bistro table until I was only a few inches from him as I held the long phallic-shaped candy between us.

"Thank you very much for the candy. This one is my favorite kind to suck on. Wanna try a lick?"

Bill's cheeks blushed darker. He cautiously leaned in towards the lollipop and opened his mouth. His eyes never left mine. He looked like a timid woodland creature approaching what he knew was a trap. I placed the tip of the lollipop in his mouth and teased it across his tongue.

"Suck it, Bill."

He closed his lips around it and slid his mouth up and down on the tip. He continued to look at me for approval as he licked. He was very intent on doing a good job. I pulled the lollipop out of his mouth and slowly slid it across his lips, using it like lipstick to paint them with the wet, sticky candy.

"How is it, Bill? Do you like the taste of my candy?"

"Uh huh! Yes. Yes. It's very good. It tastes very good."

"I'll be the judge of that."

I leaned towards him and gently licked across the front of his candy-coated lips with the tip of my tongue. He let out a slight groan and shifted in his seat.

I found it exciting to tease cute young twenty-something year-old boys until they squirmed. However, Bill was older, much older. He was in his mid-forties. When I saw him blush, babble, and squirm, I felt an entirely different level of exhilaration. I sat back in my seat and stuck the lollipop in my own mouth. I twirled it around briefly, pulled it out, then licked my deep-red colored lips.

"Mmmm. You're right. My candy is delicious."

"It's the best souvenir I've ever purchased."

"Hahaha. Yes, Bill. You made an excellent choice."

We sat and talked for a long time in that side alley off of Main Street. Bill finally relaxed after about an hour. He was a hard-working guy. He felt underappreciated in his job and lonely during the business trip. I understood that. A little bit of companionship was good for the soul.

I learned that he had never been to Walt Disney World before but he was a fan of the Wonderful World of Disney and Walt's trains. He couldn't enjoy some attractions because of his extreme motion sickness, but he obsessed over Walt's trains. His conference meetings were at the Contemporary Resort, but he was staying at the Wilderness Lodge. He spent most evenings during his trip working in the Carolwood Pacific Room of the Wilderness Lodge Villas. It was the perfect place for him to maintain his sanity when his boss pushed him too much. The room was small but was like a mini museum. It was filled with train memorabilia, including cars from the original train that Walt had in his back yard.

It had started to get dark and the crowd had thinned out a lot. It was January and chilly. There was no scheduled nighttime parade, so the park was quiet. By the time we noticed how late it was, I had finished the lollipop. It had left me with an excellent sugar buzz that encouraged me to get into some mischief.

"Didn't you say that your boss was here in the park somewhere, Bill?"

"Yeah. I'm supposed to meet him later tonight under the Main Street Train Station. He figured that I'd be in there reading the maps and posters all night anyway. He was right - that was my plan. I only left to get something to eat. Then I was distracted by you, and, well, that was even better than trains."

"You're so sweet. Thank you. Hey, I have an idea. Why don't we go for a ride on the train?"

Bill didn't question anything. He jumped up, zipped up his jacket, and followed. We walked briskly to the Train Station and went upstairs to board.

While we waited for the train to arrive, we looked around. One of the old picture-flip movie machines from the Penny Arcade now made its home there. It was the exact same one that I stalked as a young girl. It didn't even require pennies anymore. I smiled contently.

The train arrived and, not surprisingly, nobody was around. It was too cold to ride on an open train. Of course, that made it the perfect place for privacy. Bill and I climbed up into the last seat of the end-car and I huddled against him to stay warm. He was shy, but the chilly air gave him a good reason to wrap his arm around me.

The train started to move. I lifted my arms up, ran my hands up through my hair, and arched my back. I let out a long, sleepy, yawn as I stretched and pushed my breasts out in front of him. I pulled my legs up onto the seat and stretched out to lay down with my head in Bill's lap. I smiled up at him and he stared down at me with a surprised look.

"I hope you don't mind, Bill. It's been a long day for me. I'm really sleepy. It's so drafty though. I wish I had a blanket."

Bill quickly unzipped his jacket, pulled it off, and draped it over me. I tugged it up over my head as I snuggled my face down into his lap. His nervousness did not hinder his body's reaction, and I felt him grow hard against my cheek. When we were close to the Frontierland Train Station, I peeked out from under his jacket to tease him more.

"Bill, I feel something hard here next to my mouth. Do you have another unicorn lollipop for me? I wanna taste it to see if it's just as sweet."

I heard Bill moan, and I pulled the jacket back over my head. As the train stopped in Frontierland, I stayed as still as possible and pretended to be asleep. I pressed my mouth against his crotch over his pants, breathing warm air against him. As the train started back up, I unzipped his pants, pulled his hard cock through the opening, and quickly plunged my mouth fully down over it to avoid any "cold draft".

Again, he let out a moan but this time it was much louder. I couldn't help but laugh at his reaction. A few moments later, I laughed with my mouth stuffed full when I heard the recorded narrator on the train talk about the early settlers and natives. Hearing the casually-read story as I was sucking cock both amused and encouraged me.

I didn't want to make very noticeable motions, so I had little choice but to use the pressure of my tongue against his throbbing shaft. I twirled my tongue slowly up the length, then around the head over and over. I slid my lips down over him again inch by inch until I could feel the tip entering my throat. I wanted to feel that warm liquid slide down my throat and I was determined to get it. I adored feeling the hard flesh of a cock filling my mouth. It was even better than a sweet Main Street lollipop. Bill took notice of my enthusiasm. He held onto my back and kept me secure on the seat while we moved along on the track. He let me know when I hit a good spot by gripping his fingers down into me.

I knew that the train was only a few minutes away from Storybook Circus and then a few minutes more back to Main Street. This was the last loop for the train that night. I was getting off at Main Street whether or not Bill did.

We stopped at Storybook Circus and I lay there still and silent again. I held his cock in my mouth and throat, not moving at all. I felt him pet the few wisps of my red hair that dangled out from under the jacket. Again, the train movement began. The conductor spoke and I attempted to join him in the announcement.

"*Alllllll aboarrrrrd.*"

My mouth and throat vibrated as they surrounded his cock. I felt his hips rise up off the seat in response. I had to hurriedly grab on to him to keep myself from rolling off of his lap holding a mouthful of dick.

"Oh God, I love trains! I love trains so much!" He blurted out.

My tongue pressed tightly against him and I sucked him in with long, slow, strokes. I felt him swelling up more. He was ready to burst. I placed my hand on his cock and stroked up over the top of his shaft and back down again for one tight stroke before swiftly engulfing it all with my mouth.

That was all it took! Bill's balls pulsed. I could feel his legs tense up under me and hear him panting into the cold night air. He gripped onto my back while he pumped his cum down my throat. I happily drank every drop; it comforted me like warm milk on a chilly night. When his body relaxed again, I licked my lips clean and zipped him up.

The train pulled back into Main Street. I sat up and stretched once more, giving a big yawn. I handed Bill back his jacket as we disembarked from the train. An elderly gray-haired conductor greeted us as we left.

"Have a great night, folks."

"Thank you. He's a huge train fanatic. We had to get it in one last time before leaving."

"Well, I hope you enjoyed the ride, Sir!"

"Yes! Yes! I love the train! It's the best ride in the park. I could ride this all day and night. I love the train!"

I halted Bill's babbling by grabbing him by the hand and leading him downstairs. However, his blissful babbling quickly turned to concern.

"Oh, no. My boss is probably waiting. I hope he's not mad."

Bill and his boss had agreed to meet inside the covered area underneath the Train Station. We looked around and Bill spotted him almost immediately. As we approached him, he turned and leaned against the wall.

"Hey, Jack! Hope you weren't waiting too long here in the cold. We were taking a ride on the train. The train is *great*! Oh, and this is Blu. She's really friendly. She's a local."

"Pleasure to meet you, Blu."

Jack was much taller than Bill and a few years younger. He was classically handsome, standing tall and confident. I could tell immediately that he was the exact opposite of Bill: all ego. He looked down at me and flashed a cocky smile.

"Charmed, I'm sure, Jack."

"Shouldn't you be Red instead of Blu?"

Jack reached out towards me, touched one of my long locks of red hair, and twirled it around his finger. Normally, I would have smacked his hand away and explained that my name had nothing to do with the color, but, I imagined him taking that blow to his huge ego out on poor Bill for months to come. I enjoyed the time with Bill, but Jack was very easy on the eyes. Considering that I had just spent the past few hours sucking cock and lollipops, I was much more calm and agreeable. For now, boss man had my full attention.

Jack let go of my hair and touched the back of his hand to the side of my face. He trailed it down my cheek and neck, pushed my jacket open, and continued down along my breast. He never bothered to look at Bill when he spoke to him.

"You really want that promotion, don't you, Bill?"

"I... I...." Bill stammered his response.

"Epcot has Extra Magic Hours tonight. Bill, why don't you invite your pretty new friend to join us there for a nightcap?"

Jack didn't wait for a response from either of us. He took me by the hand to leave. I pulled my jacket closed as we walked out of the train station, through the Magic Kingdom exit, and up the ramp towards the Monorail.

There were only a handful of Guests waiting on the platform. Most of the crowd must have left early due to the cold temperatures and lack of evening parade. Many probably went to Epcot to have a drink and warm up like we planned to do.

We boarded the monorail to head to the Ticket and Transportation Center so that we could transfer to the Epcot monorail line. Jack sat down on one side of me with his arm propped up on the back of the seat behind me. Bill sat on my other side, quietly keeping his hands to himself. An elderly couple entered through the next set of doors down from ours, but still ended up inside our same car. They had their backs to us when they sat down, but it was still too close for comfort. No dividing walls between our sections meant that nothing much would happen on this leg of the journey.

As the monorail started to move, Jack put his hand on my chin and turned my head to look at him. He had deep blue eyes and it felt like he stared right through me. He was refreshingly bold with his intentions.

"You know I'm going to fuck you, right?"

"Yes. It's the only reason I'm here."

He took my hand in his, placed it on the bulge in his pants, and directed my hand to move up and down along the outside of the fabric. I happily obliged. If we were alone, I probably would have straddled his lap instead.

"Bill, you playing along this time?" Jack said, in a slightly condescending tone.

Bill stared out of the monorail window into mostly darkness as we approached the Contemporary Resort stop on our way to the TTC. He looked towards Jack but didn't speak. His shoulders shrugged up in an uninterested way. I decided to come to Bill's rescue.

"Jack, I don't think Bill has anything left in him after the fun we just had."

"What's that? Boring Bill nailed a broad? Nahh."

"Yes, he did. Bill's a real charmer. He already had his way with me this evening. He really knows how to treat a lady, too. He seduced me until I couldn't stand it anymore and I begged to suck his cock while we were still in the Magic Kingdom. After a few hours, he finally let me while we rode the train. It was amazing! He's exactly the kind of man that every woman dreams of."

"Well dayum, Bill! I didn't know you had it in you! It's about time I see some spunk in you. That's the kind of go-getter attitude we need in the company."

Jack beamed with pride at the thought of one of his employees acting like such a ladies' man. I turned towards Bill and gave him a wink and a smile. Bill sat wide-eyed in stunned silence.

We reached the TTC and did our monorail swap so that we were finally on the line to Epcot. This time we were sure to get an end-car that had nobody else inside. The travel time to Epcot was eight minutes or so and was uninterrupted. It was the perfect place for a quick romp.

Bill sat on one side of the car. I sat across from him on the other. Jack remained standing and leaned against one of the support poles. The message to "please stand clear of the doors," had barely ended when Jack was already unzipping his pants.

We pulled out of the station and as we went from bright florescent lighting into darkness, Jack grabbed me by the hair. In one quick motion, I was pulled to the edge of the seat and my mouth was stuffed full with his cock. He was hard as a rock and already dripping with pre-cum. He twirled his hands into my hair, gripped tightly, and fucked my face like he owned me. I gasped and struggled a bit but tried my best to keep up with the hurried pace. Boss man was the perfect ending to a night of teasing.

Bill quietly watched his boss make use of the soft, warm mouth his own dick had been in less than an hour ago. Jack yelled towards him.

"Get over here, Bill. Make yourself useful. I want that pussy soaking wet for when I'm ready to fuck." Jack pulled his cock out of my mouth and released my hair. He pushed me back in the seat and kicked my legs apart.

"Lift your skirt for me, darlin'," he ordered me in a much-sweeter tone than when he spoke to Bill.

I reached down to the hem of my dress and slowly slid it up

while I spread my legs even wider. Bill lowered himself onto the floor of the monorail. Jack and I both watched him crawl on his hands and knees towards my waiting pussy. He placed a few light kisses onto my inner thighs as he pulled down my panties. Once they were off, he shoved them into his jacket pocket and then dove in. His wet tongue eagerly lapped at my clit and teased long strokes up and down. He made me moan faster than I did for him on our train ride. I grabbed the back of his head and pushed my hips up to meet his face as he probed his tongue into me. I made sure to give him the encouragement that his boss never had.

"Good boy, Bill. Good boy. Damn. I love a good tongue-fuck."

Jack was leaning against the support pole again, stroking his dick and watching Bill service me for about a minute. I was enjoying grinding on his face and riding his tongue when Jack stepped towards me and forced my back against the seat. He opened my jacket and pulled it down over my shoulders. The top of my dress quickly followed. I heard some threads tear as he stretched it, but I've always said that all clothing was an acceptable sacrifice for hot sex.

Jack made sure that my tits were exposed for him before he straddled my lap. He pinned my shoulders to the seat and teased his cock along my cleavage, up my neck, and to my lips. I moved my head back and forth darting my tongue out, trying to taste him. Once again, he grabbed up handfuls of my hair, slid his cock between my eager lips, and fucked my face at his own rapid pace. My eyes started to water as I tried to take him all in, but I didn't really care. Bill was devouring me like an animal. I was happily distracted.

Jack pulled his cock from my mouth and trailed the tip all over my lips. In between his soft touches and smiles, he was rough and crude. He used his cock to smack at my face and mouth while he muttered his version of a compliment.

"Damn, you've got some pretty cock-sucking lips."

At that moment, vulgar dirty talk seemed appropriate for a fast monorail fuck with new friends. I looked up and smiled, but he quickly plunged back down into my throat fucking it almost as hard as Bill was pressing his face into my pussy. I moaned softly around him, trying to swirl my tongue and tease at his shaft, but he controlled it all and used my mouth as he wished.

Suddenly, the monorail shook back and forth. Jack gripped on to my hair harder to brace himself. Then he let out a sudden groan and looked down over his shoulder at Bill.

"Fuck, Bill. Is that pussy wet for me yet?"

"Uh huh."

Bill didn't bother to pull his face away from my pussy, he just mumbled as he continued tonguing me. He made every effort to impress his boss.

Jack dismounted from straddling my face and motioned for Bill to move out of his way. Jack stood in front of me and pulled my legs up in the air, then quickly tugged my body so that my ass rested on the edge of the seat. I held on to my legs so that they stayed up and spread. I was fully open and exposed for him to take either hole.

Jack held onto his dick, teased it around my clit, and rubbed it over my wet swollen pussy lips. I bit at my bottom lip, wanting him inside.

"Fuck me!" I growled at him.

He put the tip of his dick against my hole and teased it around before plunging inside me. Once he had me completely filled, he paused. For the first time, Jack spoke graciously to Bill with overwhelming praise.

"Oh my God, Bill. You did a damn fine job here, a *damn* fine job!

Before Jack could finish his accolades, a monorail recording announced that we were now approaching Epcot.

"You have *three* minutes!" I yelled.

"Bill, get over here and give a hand. I want to feel her cum all over my dick!"

Bill hurried back over towards us and lowered down on the floor between mine and Jack's legs.

The monorail tilted slightly as it curved around the part of the track that enters the park and circles around the Future World section of Epcot. Spaceship Earth filled the view out of our entire monorail window. It made for a beautiful view at night. Neither Bill nor Jack had been to Epcot during their weeklong conference trip. Jack lost his focus and stared in awe.

"*Wow*, it's the big golf ball!"

I reached up and slapped him dead-on across the face.

"It's *not* a *fucking* golf ball! It's a pentakis dodecahedron! Now hurry, fuck me harder!"

Jack put his hand to his face to soothe the sting and then leaned forward towards me. He gripped the seat behind my shoulders and started slam-fucking me. Within seconds of him starting the new pace, I felt a momentary tease of Bill's fingertip along the opening of my ass.

"Oh, fuck. Oh, fuck. I'm gonna cum!" I screamed.

I barely got the words out as Bill tilted his head under us, pushed his face to my ass and started to tongue-fuck it. My pussy immediately started to pulse and grip onto Jack's cock, soaking him as I came and screamed. Jack growled as he stared down at me smiling.

"That's it... that's it... cum for me, girl. I wanna feel it."

I heard the automated monorail announcement about Mission Space being an "exhilarating, sensory thrill-ride," just as Jack pulled out of my well-fucked pussy. He furiously stroked his wet cock. Within a few seconds, he painted my neck and tits with his cum. I closed my eyes and rubbed my hands all over myself to work the warm cream into my flesh.

Another monorail message announced that we were passing by the Land Pavilion. Jack grabbed his pants from the corner and practically jumped into them. Bill returned to his seat and brushed the dust from his knees. The glistening moisture all over his face remained. I pulled my dress down over my lap and pulled the top back up along with my jacket. My hair was a hot mess. I ran my fingers through it to straighten it as best I could, but I had always been rather fond of the freshly-fucked look. So, I didn't invest too much effort into the cause.

As we pulled into the Epcot monorail station, we all sat quietly in our seats as if nothing unusual had happened. Before we came to a complete stop, Bill and Jack stood up, ready to exit. Bill remained quiet, but Jack looked ready for a stiff drink.

"Damn, I need a drink. I can't wait to get a hold of one of those margaritas in Mexico."

"Listen, guys. I had a great time. Y'all are a lot of fun, but I'm gonna head back to the TTC to get my car. It's been a long day and well, I'm kinda... sticky. I hope you handsome gentlemen don't mind if I call it a night."

I noticed Bill lower his head. It almost looked like he was pouting. I stood up, pulled him to me by the front of his jacket, and gave him a long, deep, kiss. I enjoyed tasting myself on his lips. The monorail doors opened. I moved my hands up to hold Bill's head. I placed one light kiss on his forehead then whispered my goodbye into his ear.

"Keep the panties, Bill. You earned them big guy."

Jack and Bill both stepped off the monorail. As I sat back down, I saw Jack reach up to put his arm around Bill's shoulders. They walked off together looking like the best of friends. Before the monorail doors closed, I heard Jack's loud commanding voice when he spoke to Bill.

"Excellent performance, Bill. Let's talk about that promotion."

I leaned back into the seat and released a contented sigh.

The monorail automated announcement played again, "Please stand clear of the doors. Por favor mantengase alejado de las puertas."

The doors closed.

The monorail pulled away.

Acknowledgments

Dad
Mom
David C.
Rob D.
Daddy John
Leonard Kinsey
Effie Constantin
Steve
James H. C.
Guy Hutchinson
Bart Scott
Daniel H.
Pentakis Dodechahedron
M.H.
The Cast Members of the Walt Disney World Parks and Resorts, who appreciate the traditions, and enjoy making magic for Guests.

www.ingramcontent.com/pod-product-compliance
Lightning Source LLC
Chambersburg PA
CBHW020648260626
47157CB00008B/2959